BOOK TWO

EDGED

USA TODAY BESTSELLING AUTHOR

HEATHER SLADE

EDGED

© 2020 Heather Slade

This book is a work of fiction. The names, characters, places and incidents are products of the writer's imagination or have been used fictitiously and are not to be construed as real. Any resemblance to persons, living or dead, actual events, locale or organizations is entirely coincidental.

979-8-88649-135-7

edged

/ejd/

verb

give an intense or sharp

quality to

MORE FROM AUTHOR HEATHER SLADE

BUTLER RANCH
Kade's Worth
Brodie's Promise
Maddox's Truce
Naughton's Secret
Mercer's Vow
Kade's Return
Butler Ranch Christmas

WICKED WINEMAKERS
FIRST LABEL
Brix's Bid
Ridge's Release
Press' Passion
Zin's Sins
Tryst's Temptation

WICKED WINEMAKERS
SECOND LABEL
Beau's Beloved
Coming Soon:
Cru's Crush
Bones' Bliss
Snapper's Seduction
Kick's Kiss

ROARING FORK RANCH
Coming Soon:
Roaring Fork Wrangler
Roaring Fork Roughstock
Roaring Fork Rockstar
Roaring Fork Rooker
Roaring Fork Bridger

THE ROYAL AGENTS
OF MI6
Make Me Shiver
Drive Me Wilder
Feel My Pinch
Chase My Shadow
Find My Angel

K19 SECURITY
SOLUTIONS TEAM ONE
Razor's Edge
Gunner's Redemption
Mistletoe's Magic
Mantis' Desire
Dutch's Salvation

K19 SECURITY
SOLUTIONS TEAM TWO
Striker's Choice
Monk's Fire
Halo's Oath
Tackle's Honor
Onyx's Awakening

K19 SHADOW OPERATIONS
TEAM ONE
Code Name: Ranger
Code Name: Diesel
Code Name: Wasp
Code Name: Cowboy
Code Name: Mayhem

K19 ALLIED INTELLIGENCE
TEAM ONE
Code Name: Ares
Code Name: Cayman
Code Name: Poseidon
Code Name: Zeppelin
Code Name: Magnet

K19 ALLIED INTELLIGENCE
TEAM TWO
Coming Soon:
Code Name: Puck
Code Name: Michelangelo
Code Name: Typhon
Code Name: Hornet
Code Name: Reaper

PROTECTORS
UNDERCOVER
Undercover Agent
Undercover Emissary
Coming Soon:
Undercover Savior
Undercover Infidel
Undercover Assassin

THE INVINCIBLES
TEAM ONE
Decked
Edged
Grinded
Riled
Smoked

THE INVINCIBLES
TEAM TWO
Bucked
Irished
Sainted
Hammered
Ripped

THE UNSTOPPABLES
TEAM ONE
Furied
Merried

COWBOYS OF
CRESTED BUTTE
A Cowboy Falls
A Cowboy's Dance
A Cowboy's Kiss
A Cowboy Stays
A Cowboy Wins

Table of Contents

1

Rebel

August

"Hey, Bobby, think we could close up early tonight?" There were only a handful of people in the bar he owned and I worked at, and it looked like most were getting ready to leave. Before he could answer, a group of guys came in, every one of them already drunk off their asses.

"Fuck," Bobby muttered under his breath as we stood side by side, washing glasses. "Not these sons of bitches."

"Who are they? I've never seen them in here before."

"ABT. Every last one of 'em."

"Aryan Brotherhood?" I whispered.

Bobby turned his back to them and kept his voice real low. "Keep quiet and watch yourself, Rebel. I'm gonna go give Mac a call." Mac was Bobby's brother and the sheriff of Hays County.

I finished washing the glasses and then hollered at the guys who had just come in. "What can I get you, fellers?"

"Hell, I'll take some sugar if you're offerin'. Whaddaya think, Possum? You want some sugar too? I don't mind sharin'."

The man closest to me slowly raised his head. When our eyes met, the glass I'd been rinsing crashed to the floor and shattered.

I'd never forget those eyes. They were black as coal with hardly any white around the pupils. The last time I saw them was the night my mama died. I'd made a promise in the days that followed her death that if I ever saw them again, I'd kill the man they belonged to. *Possum.* That's what the other guy had called him, and it sure as fuck fit.

Before I could respond, Bobby came around from the back and walked to the end of the bar where I knew he kept a gun. "We're fixin' to close, boys."

"We can get 'em one for the road, Bobby." I looked directly at the black-eyed man. "What's your poison, *Possum?*" I didn't look at Bobby; I kept my gaze fixed on the bastard who'd killed my mama.

2

Edge

I had three more nights in Texas, and then I had to fly to Boston—a place I had zero interest in going, for a reason I didn't give a shit about.

If it were for work, that would be different. If there was a mission to be had, I was the first to raise my hand, more so now that I'd left the rules and regulations of MI5 behind and was a partner in the Invincible Intelligence and Security Group.

A partner's wife had first called us the Invincibles, and it took. Yeah, it sounded cocky as shit, but we all were, so what the hell?

I'd tried to get my best friend, Miles "Grinder" Stone, to come out with me tonight, but he was in what I referred to as his dark place.

The man had PTSD from a deployment and security mission in Iraq. I admired the guy enough to respect the times when he wasn't interested in socializing.

I could've invited Cortez "Rile" DeLéon, the eldest of the four partners, but that would be almost as bad as going out with my secondary school headmaster.

It wasn't as though I wouldn't know anyone at the Long Branch tonight or any other night. Most of the hands who worked on the King-Alexander Ranch, where I lived, frequented the place.

I pulled into the parking lot, surprised at how few cars were in it, and found a spot not too far from the entrance.

Climbing out of the ranch's 1957 Ford pickup I'd borrowed, I slammed the creaky door closed. The locks had a tendency to stick, so I didn't bother securing it. If any wanker tried to make off with it, this truck, like the rest of those at the ranch, was equipped with a tracking device that would allow the engine to be shut off remotely.

I hadn't done it yet, but if I was ever given the chance to, I'd press the kill button as soon as the driver hit a decent speed. For the Ford, that would be about seventy since the old thing wouldn't go much faster. I chuckled, thinking about the look on the bastard's face when the truck flipped end to end on one of the area's dirt roads.

It was hotter than Hades tonight with close to one hundred percent humidity, but I still wore my pearl snap shirt and pressed Cinch jeans. Anything else would get me tossed out of the Branch—as we affectionately called it—on my arse.

Walking past a newer edition pickup, I averted my eyes when I saw the front bench seat was occupied by a couple shagging. I was almost to the back bumper when I realized the sounds the woman was making weren't those of pleasure.

I spun around, wrenched open the door, grabbed the arsehole by the shirt collar, and pulled him away from the woman I could now tell was trying to fight the guy off.

"What the fuck?" the guy slurred.

I threw him up against the truck next to his, and as I did, I got a whiff of alcohol.

Holding the drunk by the neck, I turned around to tell the woman to get dressed and get the hell out of there, but she was ahead of me. Instead of getting out of the passenger side, she climbed out of the driver's side, walked straight over to the wanker, and slammed her knee into his crotch. I cringed, thinking about how much that had to hurt.

When she threw a punch into the guy's gut, I thought I may have fallen in love at first sight.

I heard a car pull up and looked over my shoulder, surprised to see the sheriff. "Hey, Mac. Good timing."

"What's goin' on here?"

"The fucker tried to rape me," said the woman, wiping what looked like blood from a cut on her face.

I still had the guy by the back of the collar. I let him go, and he fell to the ground, hands on his crotch.

"I got this, Edge. You go on and get outta here."

"Thanks, mate. I owe you one." In my line of work, the last thing I could afford was to be a witness in a rape trial.

I walked over to the old Ford and was about to climb in when I heard a soft voice ask me to wait. When I turned around, the feisty woman who'd slammed her would-be rapist in the balls with her knee, got on her tiptoes and planted a kiss right on my lips. It wasn't a chaste one either. "Thanks, Edge," she said as she walked away.

I shook my head and climbed into the truck, wishing I could stay, but knowing I couldn't.

Two nights later, wanting to grab a pint before I left town for God knew how long, I went back to the

Branch. It was harder to find a parking spot tonight; it looked like the place was packed.

I pulled open the heavy door and made my way through the crowd. When I got up to the bar, the owner brought me a beer before I had a chance to order.

"This one's on her." He pointed to the end of the bar.

I looked to where he motioned and met the woman's eyes. "What's her name?"

"That's Rebel."

3

Rebel

I was just finishing up my break when I saw him walk in. *Edge.* That's what the sheriff had called him. Until then, I hadn't known his name, but I'd seen him in the bar before. Each time, he hadn't paid any attention to me. Looked right through me, in fact. It wasn't that surprising; the man was hot as fuck.

I watched the exchange between him and Bobby, wondering if he'd remember me from two nights ago. When my boss pointed to the end of the bar where I was sitting, Edge raised his head and looked straight at me. His eyes were brown; mine were blue. Everybody said they were my mother's eyes. I didn't think they were that alike, other than in color. If they were similar to my father's, I wouldn't know. I'd never met the man.

I watched him walk my way. Was I ready to have a conversation with the man who'd saved me from being raped by a man I'd intended to kill?

Since my break was over anyway, I slammed down the rest of the whiskey in my glass and stood to go back behind the bar. Before I could, I felt his hand on my arm.

"Thanks for the pint," he said in his English accent. "Next one's on me."

"You're welcome." I clinked my empty glass to his, wishing I had any idea what to say to this man.

He held out his hand. "I'm Edge. But you already knew that, didn't you?"

When I introduced myself as Lucy, he looked at me funny.

"Not Rebel?"

My grandfather first called me the nickname I'd had since I was a hotheaded eleven-year-old hell-bent on making my mama's life as hard as possible.

"Come on, little Rebel," he'd said, cuffing me behind the neck with his thick hand and leading me into the house. "Let's go see if your grandmother has dinner ready."

He'd picked up my suitcase that night like it was nothing that I showed up unannounced with all my belongings.

"Yeah, Rebel," I muttered, taking a sip from the glass of whiskey Bobby set in front of me. When he winked before walking away, I sat back down on the barstool.

"Nickname?"

I nodded. "From childhood."

"My name's Keon, but I go by Edge."

As he brought his glass to his mouth, I checked out his ink. On the inside of his forearm, there was a tattoo with two names inside a heart: Annaliese and Arlo. Under them was a date: June 11, 2008.

I don't know if he caught me looking or if it was a habit, but he covered his tattoo with his hand and then leaned forward so his mouth was close to my ear. "You kissed me, Rebel."

I looked everywhere but at him.

"Lucy?"

"What?" I asked, still not looking at him.

"I liked it."

That got me to turn my head.

He took another drink of his beer and ran his eyes down the length of me. "That isn't all I like."

I crossed my legs as the heat of his words settled right between my thighs.

Edge leaned in closer to me so I could feel his breath on my neck. "You've got quite the right hook, Rebel."

I felt my cheeks turn pink. Not my most ladylike moment.

"I liked that too."

I turned on my barstool so I could see his face. "You givin' me shit, cowboy?"

He laughed. "Oh, little Rebel, nothing could be further from the truth."

No one—literally no one other than my granddad—had ever called me that. If someone had, it would've bugged the crap out of me. However, when Edge said it, I liked it. I more than liked it.

"There's something I need to tell you." The teasing lilt was no longer evident in his voice.

"Okay," I murmured, knowing his flirting had come to an end. Did he have a girlfriend? Maybe he was married. He couldn't be gay. No way.

"I'm leaving town tomorrow, and I don't know when I'll be back."

I nodded.

"You're probably wondering why I'm telling you this."

"Kinda. Yeah."

"Because if I weren't, I'd kiss you back, Rebel, a lot harder and deeper and longer than the kiss you gave me." His lips were close enough to brush the skin on my neck. "Your lips wouldn't be the only place I kissed either."

I shuddered. I couldn't help it. My panties were soaked, and my nipples were rock hard. I was seriously considering wrapping my legs around his waist, especially when I saw the size of the bulge in his jeans.

I gave him the same once-over he'd given me. The sleeves of his shirt were taut on his upper arms, and his rock-hard thighs were so big it looked like the seams of his jeans might bust open. As thick and long as his fingers were, I couldn't help but imagine that his cock would be the same. I almost came, thinking about how his massive, muscular thrusts would feel.

He nipped my earlobe, and I groaned. This man hadn't laid a hand on me, yet I was a quivering mess of need.

"When I get back, we're going to do every single thing you're imagining right now, plus all the things you've never dreamed of, Rebel."

I swear I was *this close* to pulling him out into the parking lot and stripping myself bare for him.

The front door of the bar swung open, and I could feel the hair on the back of my neck bristle. Before I could look, Edge put his hand on my arm.

"Don't turn around."

When I went to turn my head, Edge moved his hand from my arm to the back of my neck.

He put his mouth near my ear. "I told you not to turn around."

I tried to shrug his hand away, but his grip was firm.

"Hey, Bobby," I heard Edge call him over.

"Fuck," he muttered.

I tried again to look at whatever the two were talking about, but Edge wouldn't let go.

"Rebel, you get to the back storeroom and stay there until either Edge or I come and get you."

"You better take her," said Edge.

"What? *No!* What the hell is going on?"

Bobby came out from behind the bar and grabbed my arm. "Come with me."

"How the fuck did he get bail?" I heard Edge ask as Bobby pulled me in the direction of the storeroom.

I didn't care what either of them said, as soon as Edge let go, I looked over my shoulder. *Possum.* He hadn't seen me yet, but I knew I was the person he was looking for. I watched as he was intercepted—Edge on one side, Steel, the Branch's bouncer, on the other.

Possum was a big man, but he was no match for the two of them.

"This is *my* fucking fight," I seethed as Bobby pushed me into the storeroom.

"Not tonight, it isn't." Bobby slammed the door behind him. There was a padlock on the outside, and I heard it click. The fucker had locked me in.

I raced over, peered out the window, and saw Steel and Edge each take one of Possum's arms and lead him into the parking lot.

I couldn't see what happened next, and I wasn't sure I wanted to.

4

Edge
Late November

"Sod off," I said for at least the tenth time today. Without exaggerating, I'd likely muttered it over a thousand times in the last few months. My brother, Lennox, was the recipient more often than anyone else.

I flexed the fingers of my right hand. I'd only recently regained full mobility in my arm after a bullet tore its way through it. I'd been lucky, though, as Lennox reminded me on a regular basis. I was still alive.

For a while, I hadn't wanted to be. I couldn't do my job without the use of my arm, and who the hell was I if not a private intelligence operative? In my mind, nobody.

I'd suffered through three painful surgeries and three rounds of physical therapy. Starting back from the beginning each time was the most mentally debilitating. I'd done my best to keep the rest of my body as strong as it had always been, but the equipment at the rehab center was sorely lacking compared to what I had in my home gym.

That's where I was headed now—home—at least where I considered it to be: in Texas. I didn't own the house I lived in. It was on the King-Alexander Ranch, in the hills north of Austin, and up until several months ago, one of my business partners had lived in it.

When Decker Ashford got married, he moved to a nearby ranch, which belonged to the woman who was now his wife. Before I could ask, like I'd planned to, he offered to let me move in. I paid a modest amount of rent and, when I was in town, helped with chores around the ranch.

I had enough money to buy my own place. A house, at least, but living on a ranch was something I'd dreamed of since I was a wee lad. Being able to walk into a barn, saddle up a horse, and ride out on the open range was the best kind of life I could imagine.

I flexed my hand again, like I always did when I thought about things I might not be able to do as well as I once had. I didn't anticipate having trouble riding, but I wouldn't know for certain until I tried.

"I'm leaving for Boston in two days' time," said Lennox, looking over at me from the driver's seat of the vehicle he'd rented.

"Couldn't get a flight sooner?"

He didn't answer. I hadn't expected him to. While he was my brother, too often we fell into the role of parent and child. I was thirteen when our parents were killed in an automobile accident—one that almost took my life too. Lennox was eighteen at the time and became my guardian. I treated him far worse than I ever would've our father. Most of the time, he took it in stride, but given I was now in my mid-twenties, he shouldn't have to.

"Sorry," I mumbled. "Stop for a pint?"

"Sure."

He knew the way to the closest place to the ranch, so I leaned my head back against the seat and closed my eyes, remembering the last time I was at the Long Branch.

I'd met Rebel there shortly before I left Texas and spent much of my recovery fantasizing about her and how her body had responded to me. I could see her pebbled nipples through her shirt and smell her arousal when I told her how I'd kiss her if only I hadn't been leaving the next morning.

Instead, the bastard who'd tried to rape her showed up that night, and I'd been forced to teach him a painful lesson. I already hated him but more intensely now, considering he prevented me from what might very well have been the last fuck I ever had.

The parking lot was full when Lennox pulled in; we walked inside and found the bar was three-deep and it didn't look like there were any open tables. I pushed my way through, daring anyone in my path to give me reason to vent my ever-present rage.

When I got up to the bar, I didn't see Rebel, but Bobby reached over to shake my hand. I said a silent prayer it wouldn't spasm, like it did sometimes.

"Good to see you back here, Edge."

"Thanks, mate." I picked up the pint he set in front of me and took a long swig. "Keep those coming." I gestured to my brother. "Pull another one for him too, would you? Two shots of Irish while you're at it."

While I waited for him to come back with my order, I looked around but still didn't see Rebel. Should I ask about her? How much of a wanker would that make me?

Deciding the possibility of getting laid outweighed my pride, I went for it. "Where's Rebel?" I asked after Bobby set the two shots in front of me.

"You haven't heard?" he answered, scrubbing his face with his hand. "Shit," he muttered.

Why had I asked? Why had I even come here tonight? I wasn't sure I had enough alcohol in me to hear whatever it was he was about to say. I handed Lennox his pint and shot, downed the whiskey, and finished my beer. "Heard what?"

"Rebel's in jail."

"*Bloody hell.* What for?"

"Killin' Possum."

I gripped the bar, letting Bobby's words sink in. I remembered every detail of what had happened that last night I was in town. Rebel hadn't killed Possum, but I knew who had.

"Where's Steel?" I asked.

"Fucker moved to Austin."

Bobby moved away to wait on other customers, not that I planned to question him further. I'd get far more information about Rebel's arrest from Decker.

"Ready?" I asked Lennox when I saw he'd finished his pint too. It was too noisy for me to explain why I didn't want to order another.

We walked out to the parking lot in silence, and I was thankful for it. I was consumed by what had really happened that night as I got in the car and Lennox drove toward the ranch.

I checked the time on my mobile. It was a little after eight, not too late to send a text asking Decker if we could meet in the morning.

What's your twenty? he answered a few seconds later.

Ranch gate.

At the main house.

"Stop here," I said when we drove up. "There's something I need to talk to Decker about."

Lennox nodded and parked the car.

Once inside, I saw Grinder and Rile seated at the table along with Deck. With them were Quint Alexander, the ranch's owner, and his wife, Darrow Whittaker-Alexander, who also happened to be an agent with my former employer, Her Majesty's Secret Intelligence Service. I'd been with MI5, the domestic side, while Darrow, code name Shadow, was with the international MI6.

I walked over to kiss her cheek. "Hello, Shadow."

Rile stood and embraced me. It had been almost a month since I saw him in London the night before my last surgery.

He took a step back, held out his hand, and I shook it. "Good," he murmured, commenting on my grip. "Back to normal?"

I nodded, turning to Grinder. It had only been a week since I saw my best friend.

"You all right?" he asked as he embraced me like Rile had.

Grinder's eyes scrunched when I shook my head.

"Can I get you a drink?" Quint asked.

"Please. If it's not an intrusion."

"Of course not." As the son of MI6's current chief, Quint was used to impromptu meetings taking place in his kitchen.

"Lynx." Rile used my brother's code name. "Do you have an answer for us?"

"Soon. I promise."

The four original Invincibles partners—myself, Decker, Grinder, and Rile—had agreed to offer Lennox a partnership in our firm. I expected he'd join us, but first, he had some unfinished business in Boston with a woman I anticipated he'd ask to be his wife. If she agreed, I was certain he'd leave his own post with SIS and partner with us.

"What did you want to meet about?" Decker asked.

I motioned toward the kitchen, so we could talk privately. "We stopped by the Long Branch on our way here, and Bobby said there's been an arrest in a murder that took place shortly after I left."

Decker nodded. "Possum."

"That's right."

"He was found dead in the Branch's parking lot the day we flew to Boston."

I leaned back against the kitchen counter as the thoughts swirling in my head left me unbalanced. "Fuck," I muttered, not intending to say it out loud. "Come with me." I led Decker out the back door.

"What's goin' on, Edge?"

"I was there, Deck."

"What do you mean?"

"I'm the one who killed Possum."

5

Rebel

"You have a visitor, Marks," said the guard, opening the door to my cell.

"My lawyer?"

She shook her head.

I wasn't surprised to hear it wasn't him. The bastard hadn't set foot in the jail once. The handful of times I'd talked to my public defender were in court. Honestly, that was okay with me. The guy gave me the willies anyway. There was something about him that was just…creepy.

"Gotta be a mistake." I walked behind her, down the corridor to the visitation rooms, a part of the jail I'd heard about but had never been in.

She unlocked the door, and I followed her in. When I saw who was waiting on the other side of the glass partition, I wished I could turn around and walk back out.

"What are you doing here?" I asked after picking up the phone receiver the guard had pointed to when she led me to the table.

"How are you, Rebel?" asked the man I'd prayed would show up here for the first month after I was arrested. Finally, I'd given up hope, and here he was.

How was I? I was in jail for a murder I didn't commit. "Edge," I said, not answering his question.

"I heard what happened. Listen, I…" He looked on either side of him at the other visitors talking with prisoners. "I'm sorry. I was away a lot longer than I anticipated."

I shrugged. What could I say? That it was okay? It wasn't okay or not okay. It just was.

"We need to talk, and I want you to know I'm working on…things." He moved the phone receiver to his other hand and shook the one that had been holding it, like it had fallen asleep or something. "I wanted to get here right away, though. I, um, flew in last night."

"I didn't do it," I whispered, wishing I hadn't the second I did. I didn't owe him an explanation.

"I know you didn't, and I'm trying to rectify that right now."

Rectify it? What did that mean? For weeks I'd wondered if Edge had killed Possum, or maybe Steel, not that I admitted my suspicions to a soul. Had I been right?

"I've a solicitor meeting me here in an hour's time. After that, we'll see how quickly we can get in to see a magistrate." He looked left and right again. "Once the solicitor gets here, we'll be able to talk in private."

I moved the phone away from my ear.

"Wait," I heard him say before I hung it up. "I'll make this right. I promise."

I placed the receiver in the cradle and turned around to motion the guard. I looked over my shoulder one more time. When my eyes met Edge's, he mouthed, "I'm sorry."

"Busy day," said the same guard who'd escorted me out of my cell earlier. "Now it is your lawyer."

I followed her down a different corridor, this time to a room. It was empty when we entered, but a few minutes later, Edge walked in with a man I didn't recognize.

"Remove the cuffs," the man barked at the guard.

"Sir, I—"

He stalked over and shoved a piece of paper at her. "Remove them. *Now.*"

I rubbed my wrists after she did and then watched her walk out.

"I'm Sterling Anderson." He held out his hand. "Your new attorney."

Attorney? The guy looked more like a bodybuilder with a tattoo addiction. I could see them peeking out of his shirt collar and also at the end of his sleeves. His head was shaved, but his beard was full. As I studied him, he never took his eyes off me. Was he analyzing me while I did the same to him?

I ripped my gaze from him and turned to Edge. "What's going on? What about my other lawyer?"

"I hired him to represent you."

"I don't understand why the judge didn't make the PD recuse himself. He's got a goddamn tie to the vic," the Anderson guy said, shaking his head as he studied the file he held.

"I still don't understand."

"I'm working on your release. I'd prefer to schedule a hearing to have the charges against you dropped, but at the very least, I'll be getting you out on bail, pending dismissal."

Edge walked over and took my hands in his. "I'm going to confess."

I started to shake. He *had* killed him. *Fuck.* And all this time, I sat in jail, paying for a crime I didn't commit.

"Come and sit." He led me over to the table and pulled a chair around so he was sitting in front of me, our knees almost touching. I should've resisted, but I was too stunned.

"That night—"

"Hang on a minute," said the lawyer.

Edge glared at him and then looked back at me. "I didn't mean to kill him, but—"

The bald guy interrupted him again. "You didn't."

Edge shook his head. "We've been over this, Hammer. I told you what happened that night."

"You did. However, this"—he held up a thick report—"says Possum died of a gunshot wound."

Edge's eyes opened wide. *"What? Are you certain?"*

"One of the bar's employees found him the next morning, lying next to his truck. Thought he was passed out drunk until they flipped him over. Unless things happened differently than what you told me earlier, you didn't kill him." Then he looked at me. "When Edge left that night, you were still at the bar?"

I nodded.

"For how long?"

"Hammer..." Edge glared at him, but the man ignored him.

"How long, Ms. Marks?"

"They locked me in the goddamn storeroom." I glared at Edge and then turned back to the attorney. "I was in there for at least fifteen minutes when he knocked on the door and told me that Steel was going to make sure I got home okay."

"Steel?"

"The bouncer," Edge answered before I could.

"Could he have shot him?"

"Negative. He went back inside before I left."

"Could he have come back out?"

"No," I interrupted. I was the one who was still there after Edge had left. Why the fuck was he answering all the questions? "Steel followed me home and walked me in."

"Did he stay?"

"No."

"Did you go back to the bar?"

"Hammer!" This time Edge stood and banged his fist on the table. *"Stop this!"*

"I need to know, Edge. Either I ask the questions, or I walk the fuck out of here. Which is it going to be?"

Edge scrubbed his face with his hand. "Go on, then. But tread carefully."

"Did you go back to the bar?"

"No."

"Did you go anywhere else?"

"No."

"What did you do?"

"Went to bed."

"With anyone?"

Edge stalked toward the lawyer and got in his face. "Enough, Hammer," he seethed.

"Back the fuck off, Edge." He turned back to me. "Did you kill him?"

"No."

"Did you want to?"

"Yes."

"What was your motive, Ms. Marks?"

"The fucker killed my mother."

The lawyer took a deep breath, let it out, and looked at Edge. "Now you see what we're up against."

"I didn't do it." For the second time, I wished I'd kept my mouth shut, but now that I knew Edge hadn't killed him and Steel probably hadn't either, I needed to start sticking up for myself.

Both men looked at me, but only Edge spoke. "I know you didn't."

The lawyer pulled his phone out of his pocket and looked at something on the screen. "We've got our hearing."

Edge squeezed my hand. "When?"

"Three hours, which means we have a lot of work to do." He pulled out a chair and sat down at the table. "Edge, it would be best if you let me confer with my client alone."

"Bail is set at one hundred thousand dollars." The judge banged his gavel on the bench.

Great. Any hope I'd felt after meeting with the lawyer—Hammer, as he insisted I call him—vanished. I doubted I even had ten dollars in my wallet, wherever that was being kept, and in the bank, I had even less.

The tips I made tending bar at the Long Branch were decent, but before that, I'd lived paycheck to paycheck, working a crappy waitressing job at the Barton Creek Diner.

A bailiff escorted me out of the courtroom, but instead of taking me back to the jail, she took me to a meeting room like the one where I'd met with my previous lawyer. A few minutes later, she returned with a bag.

"These are your belongings. Change your clothes, and when you're ready, knock on this door and I'll come back in to take you downstairs."

"I don't understand."

"You made bail, honey."

"How?"

She shrugged. "Ask that fine-as-hell-lookin' man. Maybe he posted it."

When we walked out of the elevator and through the glass door, I could see Edge talking to Hammer. As if he sensed my approach, he turned his head and looked straight at me.

"I wish you the best," said the guard, leaving me at the door.

"Thanks," I responded, not knowing what in the hell I was supposed to do next.

"I'll be in touch," the lawyer said to me before he waved and walked out, leaving me alone with Edge.

"Ready?" he asked.

"For what?"

"We're leaving."

I motioned to the door. "Can we talk outside?"

"Of course." He motioned for me to go ahead of him. "Listen, I know you may be pissed, but it was the only way."

I lifted my face to the sun and shielded my eyes. It had been so long since I'd felt its warmth. "Pissed? About what?"

"The condition of your release. You've no reason to worry. I've a guest room, and you'll have all the privacy you need."

I loved the way he said "privacy," with a short *I* instead of a long one, but I couldn't get distracted by that right now. "What are you talking about?"

He took my arm and moved me out of the way when two other people came out the door. "Hammer was able to negotiate your release, but it had to be into my custody."

"Your custody? Are you a cop?"

"Something like that."

"But..." *What?* I had no other option. I shook my head and looked at the ground. "I guess I don't have any choice," I mumbled, once again wishing I hadn't said out loud what should've stayed inside my head.

"I'm sorry, Rebel. Truly, I am."

I looked into the brownest eyes on the face of the most handsome man I'd ever seen—forget the body I could barely tear my eyes from. Under other circumstances, as in if I wasn't facing a murder charge, I would've climbed his body like a tree. "I don't want you to think I'm not grateful."

"Let's go." He led me over to an old pickup truck and opened the passenger door. "It doesn't look like much, but it runs." He closed the door behind me and walked around the front of the vehicle. My eyes tracked him the entire way. Everything about him was so fucking hot it took my breath away.

I ran my hand over the cracked leather of the bench seat, overcome by memories that sat too close to the surface on a day like today.

"My granddaddy…" I began, fighting back tears and trying to clear my throat and find my voice. It was clogged with emotion from thinking about how, when he was alive, I'd felt protected, cared for, loved. "He had a truck like this."

He reached over and wiped away a tear I didn't realize had spilled onto my cheek. "We're going to find Possum's killer, Rebel. I promise you that."

Twenty minutes later, we drove through the gates of King-Alexander Ranch. I'd never been on the property, but I'd heard stories about it. It was even more spectacular than I imagined.

"I live in one of the ranch hands' houses," he said as we passed what I guessed was the main residence.

"This is for a ranch hand?" I gasped when he pulled into a driveway and waited for the garage door to open.

It was a miniature version of the main house, built from timber and stone. Tall windows all along the front and side gave it an airy, open look, and huge wooden posts were topped with thatched roofs covering outdoor seating areas. There was even a fireplace and outdoor kitchen. It was the nicest place I'd ever seen, outside of a magazine.

"This was the manager's before he got married and moved to a neighboring ranch." He came around and opened my door. "I'll give you a quick tour." He pushed a button to close the garage and then entered a code on a keypad. "The ranch's security systems are elaborate. I'll give you the rundown after you've had a chance to rest."

I followed him into the kitchen—my favorite part of any house—not that I'd ever seen one this grand.

The cathedral ceilings were made of unfinished wood and retained by the same massive wooden posts as outdoors. One of the interior walls was covered with stone with a cutout for the range and cupboards. There were stools set up on one side of an L-shaped island and more at a breakfast bar.

We swept past the family room that was adjacent to the kitchen, and down a hallway. Edge stopped, reached around me, and opened the door.

"This is the gym. You're more than welcome to use it. It's obvious you take good care of yourself," he said as his eyes swept my body.

Not able to resist, I did the same to his. Buff didn't begin to describe him. Every muscle I could see was defined, as I anticipated was true of those I couldn't see. Edge was taller than me. He would be even if I wore heels. I liked that. A lot. His hair, that he kept closely cropped on the sides, was a mess of curls on top, and while it was brown like his eyes, both were entirely different colors. His hair was chocolaty while his eyes were caramel. Dark stubble covered his square jaw, but through it, I could see his dimples as he grinned at my blatant perusal.

Edge cleared his throat and continued to the next door which opened to a bedroom.

"The lavatory is right across the hall." He stopped smiling and scrubbed his face with his hand. "It didn't occur to me that you might need to stop and pick up some things."

I didn't have much in the way of possessions. The idea that after my arrest my asshole landlord had probably trashed what little there was, made me sick to my stomach. The photos of me with my mother and grandparents were what I mainly cared about.

Edge led me back out to the family room. "We can go out later if you'd like."

I pulled out my dead cell phone. "You don't happen to have a charger that would work with this, do you?" As soon as the words left my mouth, it occurred to me that I wouldn't have service since my bill hadn't been paid since I was arrested.

No clothes, no phone, no money. I had nothing, and considering I was out on bail with a murder charge looming, who would give me a job? I doubted even Bobby would, especially since his brother was the sheriff.

The magnitude of my dire situation landed heavily on my shoulders. "Excuse me," I mumbled, rushing back down the hall to the bathroom. Once inside, I sat on the toilet seat and wrapped my arms around my stomach as silent sobs racked my body. The truth was, I was better off in jail. At least there I didn't need to worry about my next meal or where I'd sleep or that I didn't have a cell phone. I knew it sounded crazy, even in my thoughts, but I had to ask Edge to take me back.

I turned on the faucet and let the cool water run over my wrists. It had always settled me when anxiety threatened to turn into a full-fledged panic attack. I doubted any amount of water could stop one from coming on now.

"Rebel...Lucy...are you all right?" I heard Edge ask from the other side of the door.

"I'll be right out." I splashed cold water on my blotchy, tear-streaked face while trying to figure out how to ask someone who had posted bail on my behalf to take me back to lockup.

6

Edge

I leaned against the wall, wishing I knew how to handle this situation better. Would it help if she had another woman to talk to? It occurred to me that I should've stopped at the main house and introduced Rebel to Shadow.

Returning to the kitchen, I sent her a text explaining the situation, which Shadow immediately answered, asking what I thought Rebel might need. Need? God, I was a wanker. The woman was wearing the same clothes as when she was arrested. Not to mention her apartment was surely rented by now. Who knew what might have happened to her belongings? When I responded, she told me to bring Rebel to the house as soon as it was convenient.

I heard the bathroom door open and raised my head. The rays of the setting sun streaming in through the windows shone brightly on Rebel, making her look even more beautiful than I remembered. Long, wavy brown hair framed the delicate features of her face, and her blue eyes mesmerized me as much today as they had the night we met.

While she wasn't as tall as me, her legs still looked miles long in the tight black jeans she had tucked into black military-style boots. The thin black shirt she wore, exposed a hint of her tummy, and what little I could see of it, looked as ripped as mine used to be—before I spent several weeks not doing much more than sitting on my arse.

"Hey," she said, pushing up the sleeves on her black denim jacket. "Sorry about that. I had a little bout of self-pity. Which leads me to…I appreciate everything you've done for me, Edge. Getting me out of jail and all, but the truth is…I don't know how to say this."

"Just say it." I walked closer, shoving my hands into my pockets to stop from reaching out to touch her.

"Okay…well…I need to go back."

I couldn't help myself. I took my left hand out of my pocket and brushed her hair from her face. "Back where?"

She bit her bottom lip. "To the jail."

"Why? Did you leave something there?"

She shook her head. "I just need to go back."

Thinking that maybe whatever she wanted to return for was something she didn't want to talk about, I agreed to take her without asking any more questions.

"I need to stop by the main house before we head into town." I pulled up, cut the engine, and walked around to open her door. "Come on. There's someone I want you to meet."

"Edge…"

I took her hand and pulled her out of the truck. "It'll only take a minute, after which we'll run your errand."

"Errand?"

"You know, whatever you need from the jail."

"I think you misunderstood—"

"It's okay. Whatever it is, you don't have to tell me."

"Hey, Edge," I heard Shadow holler as she came down the steps of the front porch. "You must be Rebel."

"This is Shadow—Darrow. Darrow, this is Lucy… Rebel." I was embarrassed. "I'm sorry, which do you prefer?"

"Rebel."

"It's nice to meet you, Rebel," said Shadow. "Please come in. Edge tells me that you need a few things to tide you over."

"I don't understand." She looked between me and Shadow, who tucked her arm through Rebel's and led her inside.

"Listen, when I first visited the ranch, I had nothing 'appropriate to wear,' in the words of my dear husband. Fortunately, my sister-in-law had closets full of clothes that fit me perfectly. You look to be about my size too."

Rebel stopped in the middle of the hallway and turned around to face me. "Thank you, but I'm going back to jail. To stay." Her cheeks flushed red when I stepped closer.

"You don't need to worry about that. Before this goes to trial, me and the boys will figure out who killed Possum. You aren't going to spend another day behind bars. I promise."

"Will you excuse us?" she said to Shadow; I followed her back out to the front porch.

"I know this may be hard for you to understand or even fathom, but I have nothing, Edge—literally nothing. Understand? I have no family, no home, no money. I don't have any clothes other than what's on my back. I don't even know where my car is. For all I know it's been—"

Not knowing how else to stop her from talking, I grasped the back of her neck and covered her lips with mine like I'd wanted to the night we met. I pushed my tongue into her mouth and her back up against the porch post.

Once I started, I didn't want to stop. For the last few weeks, thinking about kissing her got me through most days. Imagining that one day I'd come back and do to her body all the things I'd wanted to that night, kept me moving forward when I felt like giving up.

I kissed her cheek, her temple, her eyelid, and rested my forehead against hers. "You're not as alone as you think, little Rebel. You've got me, and with me come my friends."

"You hardly know me," she whispered. "Why are you doing this?"

"Tell you what. We'll go back inside, let Shadow pack up a bag to tide you over until we can find out where your car, along with the stuff you left in your apartment, ended up. After that, we'll take a ride and I'll answer your question. Okay?"

It took a while, but eventually, she nodded after I brought my lips to hers in another kiss.

"I can't tell you how much I've wanted to kiss you."

"Me too," she whispered, burying her face in my shoulder.

"There's so much more…" I kissed her one more time before pulling her back toward the house.

"I took the liberty," said Shadow, meeting us inside the door with a packed bag. "You'll need to go into town for some essentials, but at least you won't need to buy a whole new wardrobe."

"Thank you so much. I'll…um…get it all back to you as soon as I can."

"No need. The clothes are yours to keep."

"I can't…"

Shadow squeezed Rebel's hand. "Please. Let us do this. Quint told me what happened. The guys"—she looked at me, smiled, and winked—"the Invincibles will find out who killed that man, and you'll be able to put all this behind you."

Rebel's eyes met mine, and I knew part of explaining why I was helping her meant I also needed to tell her what I did for a living.

When she said that I hardly knew her, she was right. Just because I'd spent weeks fantasizing about her, didn't mean she was anything like the woman I'd invented in my head. Only time would tell who she truly was, and the way things appeared now, we'd have a lot of it. Conversely, she didn't know me either.

"Edge, I'm not sure how to say this," she began once Shadow left us on our own.

"I told you before. Just say it."

"I don't have any money. I know I told you that already, but I'm not sure you understand that I literally have no money. None, and I highly doubt I could get my old job back."

"One thing at a time, okay?"

"But—"

I wrapped my hand around the back of her neck.

"Are you going to kiss me every time you don't want to hear what I have to say?"

I laughed and dropped my hand. "It isn't about not wanting to hear it. It's about not wanting you to worry. Please, let me help you. I know you don't have money. I'm not concerned about it."

"But…"

"Yes?"

Rebel looked down at the ground. "I was kind of hoping you'd interrupt me again."

"Gladly." I kissed her again. "I could do this all day. Not that there's much left of it." I wrapped my arm around Rebel's shoulders and led her over to the truck. "Let's get you…what did Shadow say?"

"Essentials."

"Like…knickers, for example?" I winked.

"Exactly."

Probably wouldn't do if I told her now that I'd rather she not wear them. Ever.

Two hours later, essentials purchased, including several pairs of the aforementioned ladies' under-garments as well as a toothbrush, paste, and other womanly sundries, my mind was still on the knickers. A particular pair, in fact. Red lace and quite skimpy. Thin enough that I could easily rip them from Rebel's body with my teeth.

"Maybe we should do this tomorrow." She stifled a yawn after I suggested we run by her old apartment.

"If you'd like. On the other hand, I reckon it might be nice to have it done with."

"I bet you could talk anyone into anything with that smooth English accent of yours."

"I've no interest in talking anyone into anything. Other than you, of course."

"And what, exactly, do you want to talk me into?"

I reached across the seat and took her hand in mine. "It's more what I want to talk you out of." I pulled up in front of the address Hammer had given me and tried my best to hide my dismay. Dreadful didn't come close to describing the place Rebel used to call home.

"There it is!" she screeched, jumping out of the truck and running across the lawn. I got out and followed her to an empty parking lot, with the exception of a lone vehicle, which looked as though it hadn't run in decades. By the time I caught up, Rebel was reaching under the wheel well.

"What are you doing?"

"Looking for this." She smiled and held up a key.

I stepped back so she could unlock the door, but she didn't. Instead, she went to the boot.

"Thank God," I heard her murmur before I peeked around to see what gave her such relief. "He put it all in here. At least he didn't throw it in the garbage."

I stood back and watched as she ran her hand over the small amount of possessions as though they were the finest treasures in the universe. She picked up a framed photo and hugged it to her.

"Who is that?" I asked.

She held it out so I could see.

"Is that you and your mum?"

"Yes." She studied the photo, running her fingertips over the image. "I was seven when this was taken."

"Do you have any others?"

She sifted through the box and pulled out two more. In one she looked younger and in the other, much older. It didn't look as though it was taken that long ago.

"When was this?" I asked, peering over her shoulder.

"I was eighteen." Rebel shook her head. "It feels like a lifetime ago."

I knew from the dossier I'd asked Decker to put together that Lucy "Rebel" Marks was twenty-four years of age, yet she considered six years a lifetime. Lord knew what struggles she'd endured in that time.

I'd looked away, and when I turned back and my eyes met hers, all I could think was that I didn't want this precious girl to have to endure a minute more of hardship. I couldn't explain why, given that prior to now, all I'd thought about was getting her starkers. Maybe it was because after my parents died, I'd felt as alone as she must be feeling. I had Lennox, though. Rebel didn't have anyone. When Hammer was questioning her, she'd said that Possum killed her mother. Odd that there wasn't anything in the dossier about her mother's death. It was something I'd follow up with Decker about.

"Why are you being so nice to me?" she asked, barely above a whisper.

"I promised you a story, didn't I?"

She nodded.

"First, what shall we do with…this?" I waved my hand at her car.

"Susan."

"What?"

"My car's name is Susan."

"Your car has a name?"

"She does."

"All right, then. What shall we do with…Susan?"

She climbed inside and put the key in the ignition. There was a clicking sound, but it didn't start.

"Dead battery, most likely," I told her. "We can take care of it tomorrow."

Rebel nodded and climbed out of the car. While she locked it up, I repacked the things she'd taken out of the boxes.

"What are you doing?" she asked when I lifted the first out of the boot.

"Taking this to the truck. Be right back."

"Edge?" she shouted as I walked away.

I turned around. "Yeah?"

"Thank you."

She was quiet on the way back to the ranch, but I sensed finding her belongings had given her a certain amount of comfort.

I pulled through the gates and drove past the main house. Typically, I'd stop and check in before driving the rest of the way to my place, but tonight, Rebel and I needed to talk.

"Hungry?" I asked when I led her into the kitchen from the garage.

"Starving."

"Me too," I said, feeling like a wanker for not thinking of it sooner. "I don't have much, I'm afraid."

She walked over and stood behind me when I opened the refrigerator. "No, you don't." She reached around and grabbed a handful of items and set them on the counter. "Pantry?" she asked, putting her hand on the doorknob.

"Yes."

"Wow. You can walk in it," she gasped. Less than two minutes later, she brought more things out and set them on the counter with the items from the fridge.

"What are you doing?"

"Making us dinner."

"You don't have to do that."

She looked into my eyes and smiled. "And if I don't, what will we eat?"

"Right." I stepped out of her way.

"Besides, who wouldn't want to cook in this kitchen?"

I raised my hand as I took a seat on one of the barstools, and she laughed.

"Wow," I said, thirty minutes later after taking a bite of what she'd made. "This is brilliant."

"Thanks," she murmured. "I love to cook."

"Cook? God, woman, you should be a chef." When her cheeks turned pink, I knew I was onto something. "Is that what you'd like to do?"

She looked away. "Not that it's an option, but yeah."

I made a mental note to hunt down Tee-Tee tomorrow. She ran the ranch dining hall; perhaps she could use some help. Fall calving season had come to an end, and my guess was the cook could use a break. Another bonus? Rebel could earn some money.

The money didn't matter to me. I had more of it than I knew what to do with. I was more concerned about Rebel's pride. I sensed it was difficult for her to accept my help earlier when we were shopping for her "essentials."

I took another bite of my dinner, groaning over its goodness. Thinking about those red lace knickers only made my groans more pronounced.

"You said you were going to tell me a story."

"And I shall." When I stood and took her plate, she stood too. "Sit down and let me clean up. While I do, I'll explain a few things that may seem mysterious."

"I can help."

"Sit down," I said again, using my sternest voice.

She smiled. "All right, all right. Jeez."

"Earlier," I began, "when we were chatting with Shadow, she mentioned the Invincibles."

Rebel nodded.

"It's a firm I work for. Actually, I'm part owner. We do private security and intelligence work. Prior to that, I worked for MI5. Do you know what that is?"

Her eyes opened wide. "Like James Bond?"

"Essentially." I rubbed the back of my neck with my hand. "This part is harder to say."

"Just say it," she said with a wink.

"You asked me why I was helping you." I finished washing the pot she'd used to cook our dinner, set it down, and gripped the counter with my left hand. "When I left in August, I didn't know at the time, but it was for work. During that mission, I was shot. It had been a black op to extract an MI6 agent and a British diplomat who had been kidnapped by the Chinese government. We were minutes from making it out unscathed when I was hit."

"Oh my God."

I raised my right hand which, thankfully, was still. "The bullet went in here." I pointed to my upper arm. "It did considerable damage, requiring more than one surgery. Three to be exact. After the first two, I still didn't have full use of it."

"I don't know what to say."

"Nothing to say. Except maybe to ask me what this has to do with my helping you."

"Why are you?"

I dried my hands on the towel and walked around the breakfast bar. I spun her stool so she was facing me, put my hands on her knees, and spread her legs. "Because every day, when I thought about giving up, it was the idea that I'd one day do this, that kept me going." I leaned forward and kissed her the way I'd told her I would the night at the Long Branch.

Rebel opened her mouth to me, and I plunged my tongue inside, thrusting it like I planned to do when I was finally between her legs, with both my mouth and my cock.

She whimpered and grasped both cheeks of my arse, pulling me closer to her. She scooted forward on the stool, and I was at the right height that, when she did, she could grind her pussy against my hardness.

"Imagining fucking you, putting both of my hands on your body, was the incentive I used every day."

"God, Edge," she groaned.

"Tell me, little Rebel, did you think of me at all?"

7

Rebel

Yeah, I thought about him. Like he'd said, the idea that I'd see him again someday kept me going. As long as I didn't think too far into the future, the fantasy of him swooping in and breaking me out of jail recurred almost daily. While he hadn't broken me out, here I was, sitting in his kitchen, only because he'd come to get me.

Would telling him that scare him off? My experience with men led me to believe it would. Anytime I'd mentioned seeing someone again, it was the last time I did.

"Tell me what you thought about, Rebel. If you did."

"I did." I could barely speak I wanted him so much.

Our eyes met, and the look he gave me sent a shot of lust straight to my clit. The red lace panties I couldn't wait to put on since I saw the look on his face when I added them to my purchases, were now drenched.

Edge kissed me again, this time sliding his hand under my shirt. "Is this okay?" he whispered.

"Yes," I moaned. "More than okay." Merely having his hand on my skin sent a scorching shudder through my body.

"Do you have any idea how much I wanted you that night? How much I want you right now?" His accent sent shivers down my already quivering spine.

I closed my eyes and took a deep breath. Was this going to happen? I'd wanted Edge to fuck me since the first time I laid eyes on him, but what would happen after he did? I was a murder suspect, facing trial. I had nowhere to live, except with him. And it wasn't that I was just living with him; I was in his custody. Would things be too awkward after we had sex? Would he want me to leave as much as I would feel like I should?

"Wait." I pushed him back so our bodies were no longer touching.

"Wait? I've waited three painfully long months to be with you, Rebel."

"But..."

Edge's face changed; instead of heated, it looked... disappointed. "If you're saying no, I will respect that."

I bit my bottom lip, wondering if I was making the wrong decision. What if he asked me to leave because I wouldn't have sex with him?

"Little Rebel." He cupped my cheek with his palm.

"I'm saying…not yet."

He brought my hand to his lips and kissed the back of it. "Let me ask you this."

I raised my eyebrows.

"Can I still kiss you?"

"Sure, we can still kiss."

He turned my hand over and brought his lips to my wrist. "Here?"

"Yes."

He pushed the sleeve of my jacket out of his way and kissed the hollow on the inside of my elbow. "What about here?"

My eyes drifted closed as another shudder ran through my body. Saying no to this man was going to be the death of me.

"Rebel?" He kissed the same sensitive spot again, this time opening his mouth and pressing the hard tip of his tongue against it.

"Yes."

He brushed my hair out of his way and kissed my neck, right below my ear.

"Yes," I groaned before he asked.

"And here?" He touched my temple with his lips and then kept going, kissing across my forehead, my eyelids, my other temple, and below my other ear.

He had to know how turned on I was. Had to. He also had to know how close I was to changing my mind and dragging him to the nearest bed.

He kept going, down my other arm, to the hollow of the inside of my elbow, to my wrist, and finally, to the back of my hand.

"Come with me." He pulled me from the stool and led me down the hallway. I figured he knew that my resolve was long gone and even though I'd said no before, this time I wouldn't.

He opened the door of the bedroom where we'd put my packages, walked over to the bed, and picked them up. I watched with curiosity as he took them farther down the hallway.

"Rebel?" he said, turning around. He motioned with his head for me to follow.

I stepped into what I guessed was his bedroom. The king-size bed was on a platform and covered by a copper and black spread that matched the mottled walls of the room. Shelves full of books flanked each side of the bed, and at the foot, there was a leather-upholstered bench that matched the headboard. It was exactly how I would've described the room of the man currently dropping my packages on the end-of-the-bed bench. He walked past me and, a minute later, came back, carrying one of the boxes we'd found in the trunk of my car.

"What are you doing?"

"Moving you."

"So now I'm sleeping in here with you?"

After setting the final box on the bench, he walked over and cupped my cheek. "You are sleeping in here, yes, but not with me. You said 'not yet,' and I told you I would respect your wishes."

"But—"

He quieted me with a kiss that rocked me from my lips all the way to my toes.

"After what you've been through the last several weeks, I want to pamper you. And while I happen to think my bed is the most comfortable I've ever slept in, that isn't what's most special about this room."

He led me over to the fireplace and flipped a switch. "In case you get cold," he said before opening a door that led into the nicest bathroom I'd ever seen. It even outdid the ones I'd seen in magazines.

Three steps up led to a bathtub large enough to hold two people comfortably. It was set into black and white marble that matched the floor as well as the sinks in the double vanity.

Across the room was a shower that, like the tub, could easily fit two people. Behind the double glass doors, there were two showerheads and two benches on either side. Those and the walls were made from the same marble as the rest of the bathroom.

"The best part is the radiant heat," he murmured.

"What is that?"

He pressed a button on a panel that looked way too complicated for me to ever figure out how to use, and then took my hand, pulling me into the shower with him.

"Feel." He rested my hand on one of the benches.

"It's warm!"

"Exactly. The floor and the walls heat too."

"Why are the walls heated?"

His eyes flamed. "Better to show you sometime."

I stepped out of the shower enclosure and walked out of the bathroom. "Edge, this is nice of you, but I can't let you give up your bedroom. Believe me, the guest room is far nicer than any bedroom I've ever slept in."

"You can and you will," he said in a tone of voice that, once again, sent heat coursing through my veins.

He walked over to another door that led to a walk-in closet. "There's plenty of room for your things in here. Several of the drawers are empty."

"But—"

He crossed the room in a flash and captured my mouth with his. After another deep, panty-melting kiss, he rested his forehead against mine. "I'm beginning to enjoy your protests very much."

"Me too." I wished he'd kiss me again. In fact, if he wanted to keep kissing me, I wouldn't stop him.

"Little Rebel," he murmured, backing away from me. "Get some rest. It's been a long day."

"Edge?" I said before he could walk out the door. "Um…could you maybe show me how to use the shower?"

He smiled. "Of course."

By the time he went through everything the shower could do, I decided a bath would be far less complicated, and maybe more relaxing.

"Enjoy, beautiful girl." He kissed my cheek and left me alone in the space that should be his.

He hadn't said so, but the tub had radiant heat too and soft water that glided over my skin. Figuring I'd never have another opportunity like this, I luxuriated until my fingers and toes were pruny, turning the jets on for the last few minutes.

I climbed out and grabbed the towel that Edge had put on the warmer for me. This was all so far over the top, and for a ranch hand's house, no less.

I pulled a cozy nightie out of one of the shopping bags, thinking I should put things away tonight, but the promise of the bed that Edge said was the most comfortable he'd ever slept in was too tempting.

I opened one of the boxes, though, and pulled out the three framed photos of me with my mother, hoping he wouldn't mind if I set them on the bookshelves, temporarily of course. I rummaged deeper and found one other photo. It was of me with my grandparents, taken shortly after I'd gone to live with them.

I hugged the photo to my chest before setting it on the shelf alongside the others. While I didn't understand my mother's inability to care for me at the time, I did now. I couldn't imagine having a kid, and I was four years older than my mother was when she'd had me.

I studied the last image taken of the two of us, so grateful that we'd had that time together. For what felt like the briefest of moments, I'd let go of my anger long enough to have a relationship with her. And she'd let go of the drugs. Until that night…I closed my eyes and pushed the memory from my head. If I dwelled on it, I'd have nothing but nightmares.

I set the photo on the shelf, climbed into bed, and hugged the pillow close to me, imagining it was Edge beside me. Not necessarily for sex, although my lady bits were cursing me for turning him down.

I knew it was silly, but I found myself wanting to tell him about my grandparents and my mom. In reality, he probably wouldn't be interested, but my pillow Edge would listen with rapt attention, wanting to know everything about me.

I rubbed my aching nipples, only one part of my body that was screaming at me for my foolish decision, imagining how Edge's mouth would feel soothing them. Soon my hand was between my legs, imagining his fingers were inside of me instead of my own.

8

Edge

I heard the jets go on in the master bath and adjusted my trousers to better accommodate my growing cock. Only seconds ago, I'd talked that part of my anatomy down from the precipice of raging desire.

As ridiculous as it would've sounded had I said it aloud, I found myself glad that Rebel had put a governor on the accelerator of the two of us having sex. I was enjoying the anticipation of our slow, deep kisses, knowing that each part of her body she allowed me to touch with my lips, would excite me so much more than if we'd rushed into shagging.

As for Rebel, I planned to torture her in the same way she was me. When I did, finally, feel her naked body beneath mine, I would bring her to the brink of ecstasy again and again before I actually let her come. My last name, Edgemon, wasn't the only reason I'd been given my code name, after all.

I locked myself in the modest guest bath, climbed into the shower, and while I imagined the jets of the other tub pulsating between Rebel's legs, I brought myself temporary relief.

When I ventured out of the bedroom the next morning, it was mainly because the heavenly smells wafting from the kitchen were more than I could resist.

I was surprised Rebel didn't hear my approach, but understood once she turned around and I saw she was wearing earbuds.

"Sorry." She pulled one bud out. "I saw these on the counter and like to listen to music while I cook."

"No apology necessary. What divine thing are you whipping up so early this morning?"

"I'm sorry," she said a second time. "Did I wake you?"

I walked over and removed the second bud from her ear and cupped both of her cheeks with my hands. "Stop apologizing. It was like a dream come true, not only to have the scent of breakfast wake me from my…ahem…erotic dream, but also to open the bedroom door to find you're truly here."

A timer went off, and Rebel twisted out of my arms and pulled a pan from the oven. "Cinnamon rolls."

If the guys in the dining hall got a whiff of these, the line for firsts, seconds, and thirds would be never-ending. "I had an idea last night that I'd like to run by you."

"Okay," she responded with a furrowed brow.

"It's something you'll like. At least I think you will." Her cheeks turned pink.

"There may be a job opening in the ranch kitchen—"

"Seriously?" she said before I could explain further.

"I'll confirm with the head cook, but I believe so."

"That would be amazing, but…"

I took the potholders still covering her hands off, set them on the counter, and pulled Rebel into my arms. "But?"

"I doubt they'd want to hire someone who's been accused of murder."

"I had a feeling that's what you'd say. However, you met Shadow yesterday. Do you think she would've been so welcoming, so generous, had she believed there was a murderer in her house?"

"She was being kind because of her friendship with you."

"While there is a certain expectation that you'd feel the way you do, how about you trust me instead?" I saw her eyes scrunch and regretted my tone of voice. "All I'm saying is that I know these people. Innocent until proven guilty is a belief they hold dear."

"Sorry, but personal experience has taught me that people aren't so quick to believe the good when the bad is so much easier."

"Does this mean you're mad at me?"

She put one hand on her hip and cocked her head. "Why would you ask that?"

"Because you're standing between me and those cinnamon buns. In a moment's time, I will likely start drooling. Although that may have less to do with the baked goods as it does with how hot you look with flour on your cheek."

She flushed again, looked away, and stepped aside. "Have at it."

Since she wasn't looking, I did, but not at what she was suggesting. Instead, I wrapped one arm around her waist and kissed her—deep and hard.

Her mouth opened to mine, and I took full advantage, my tongue sliding against hers as we waged a battle of lips, teeth, and will. I wanted this woman more than I'd ever wanted any other, and while I'd never renege on my promise to respect her wishes, I'd give anything to hear her ask me to fuck her here and now.

"Touch me," she groaned, taking my hand and sliding it under her shirt.

"Like this?" I asked, sliding my fingers under her bra and pushing the cup out of my way.

"Harder," she begged when I pinched her nipple between two fingers.

"Gladly." I pinched harder, twisting until her breath caught and I heard her gasp. I backed her up against the counter, grinding my straining cock against her, and then leaned down, nipping through the lace of her bra. At the same time she yelped, she pulled my head closer.

"That's my Rebel. You like it rough, don't you, sweetness?"

Her only answer was to groan again and rub the wetness I could feel seeping through her knickers against me. I switched my hands, held her by the arse, and slid my right hand under her shirt. Before I could torture her other nipple, my hand spasmed. *Bloody hell.* The moment ruined, I pulled away.

"What happened?" she asked, looking as bewildered as I expected she should.

I walked out of the kitchen toward the garage, muttering, "Nothing," as I left.

Instead of fondling the breasts of a woman who didn't want to have sex with me anyway, I should be working out, strengthening the weakened muscles, not just in my hand but in the rest of my body. I couldn't afford to be lax, or something far worse would happen than not being able to pinch a nipple.

I got in the truck and drove up to the barn. What I needed now more than anything was to saddle up a horse, ride out, and get a handle on my mood before I made things worse with Rebel.

The woman had enough on her mind, enough to worry about, without me acting like a horse's arse.

Instead of getting out, I put the truck in reverse and drove back to the house. I got out and stalked in the back door, where I found Rebel straightening the kitchen.

"Fancy a ride?" I asked, trying to seem nonchalant when all I sounded was angry.

"A ride?"

Where did my mind immediately go? Imagining her straddling me, riding my cock as I slammed into her, thrust after thrust.

"Horseback," I muttered, about to look away when I noticed her pebbled nipples. "Look, Rebel, I'll admit I'm a first-rate wanker, but being around you, especially after spending so much time thinking about you—"

"I feel the same." She leaned against the counter behind her and folded her arms, perhaps in an effort to cover her hardened nipples. "Long before you ever noticed me, I wanted you, Edge. Long before."

I took two steps forward, almost close enough to touch her, but not quite. "What are you talking about?"

She took a deep breath and slowly let it out. "The first time I saw you and your friends at the Long Branch, I wondered what it would be like to fuck you."

I took the same deep breath she did, steeling myself against tossing her over my shoulder, carrying her into the bedroom, and showing her exactly what it would be like. I was about to take another step forward when my mobile chimed a sound that meant the call was work-related.

"Sorry, I have to take this." I walked back out to the garage. "Hello, Decker," I answered. "What can I do for you?"

"Mac and I found something on Possum."

"Yeah?" I'd planned to call John "Mac" MacIver myself tomorrow. He wasn't just the sheriff; he was a friend. He was also the best resource when it came to local criminals.

"He was involved in some dirty shit. I think you should take a look at what we dug up."

"Where are you?"

"Home."

"Is Mac still with you?" I wasn't sure how Rebel would feel coming face-to-face with the man who had arrested her.

"Nah, he got a call and left."

"Should I head over now, then?"

"Yep. Come to Brandywine and bring Rebel with you."

Brandywine was the name of the ranch Decker's wife, Mila, had inherited shortly before they got married. It bordered the King-Alexander Ranch. On a day as nice as this one, I'd usually ride over on horseback. However, that might be too much for Rebel. Maybe she didn't like to ride at all.

When I went back inside, the kitchen was clean and she wasn't in it. I walked down the hallway and rapped on the closed bedroom door, but she didn't answer. A few seconds later, I heard the water running. I turned, rested my back against the wall, and looked up at the ceiling. It appeared I'd be taking another shower soon myself, if only to relieve the ache in my cock from knowing that, at this very minute, Rebel would be stripping naked and climbing into a bathtub big enough that I could show her what I'd wanted to do to her before Decker's call.

I nearly jumped out of my skin when the door opened and Rebel's hand sneaked out, grasping mine.

"Edge," she murmured. "I was wondering if you'd mind helping me with something?"

"Right. Of course." I pushed the door open to find her wrapped in one of the large bath sheets. "Trouble with the tub?"

"Something like that."

I motioned for her to go in front of me and adjusted my trousers as I followed. She walked over to the tub that looked to be about three-quarters full. "Do you need help with the jets?"

She shook her head.

"What, then?"

She dropped the towel. "Would it be too much trouble to ask you to wash my back?"

9

Rebel

72

I stood naked before him, shoulders back, breasts thrust forward, and waited while he looked me up and down and then back again.

"You are spectacular," he said in the accent that added to the wetness already trickling down my leg. "Come here." He held out his hand, and I walked over to him. "If I do as you ask, I might get wet."

I nodded. "Yes."

"Perhaps I should remove my clothes?"

"Yes," I repeated.

"Do it, Rebel."

His demanding tone of voice was nearly my undoing. Instead of removing his clothes, I wanted to rip them from his body. When I rested my hands on his chest, trying to stop them from shaking, Edge covered them with his.

"I need to know you want this, Rebel."

"I do." I grasped the hem of his shirt and lifted it. Edge raised his arms, and I pulled it over his head.

"Now my trousers," he rasped.

I slid his workout pants over his hips and gasped when his erection popped free. As I'd expected when I looked at his hands and pictured his cock, it was long and thick.

"Finish," Edge demanded as I knelt in front of him and he stepped out of his pants, leaving him naked other than his socks. I slipped each one off and then, still on my knees, looked up at him. He put his hands under my arms and lifted me to my feet. "As much as I long to feel your sweet mouth on my cock, I want you so much I wouldn't last." He pulled me toward the bathtub. "Get in."

As I climbed over, I felt his fingers skim my slit and had to hold on to the edge as I eased into the warm water. I sat and waited for him to join me. Instead, he picked up a bottle of body wash and squeezed some of the liquid into his hands.

"Lean forward."

I groaned when his powerful fingers massaged my achy muscles.

"Feel good, little Rebel?"

"So good."

As much as I wanted him to keep rubbing my back, I wanted to feel his hands all over my body more.

I looked into his eyes. "Aren't you coming in?"

"I told you. I need to know you want this. You want it, you say it, and I'll do it."

"Get in."

He smiled, and heat flashed in his eyes. "Yes, ma'am." He pushed me forward and slid in behind me, picked up the body wash, and squeezed more into his hands, this time massaging the foaming liquid into my breasts.

"God, I love your tits," he muttered. I could feel his hardness poking into me and shifted. "Get back here," he said, lifting me and putting his legs together so I was seated on his lap, his cock now nestled between the cheeks of my ass.

Edge drizzled more of the body wash on my stomach and, when he set the bottle down, used his hands to spread it lower. He rested one hand on my mound and brought the other around the back of my thigh and thrust two fingers inside of me while the fingers of the other hand toyed with my clit.

If he didn't have a strong hold on me, I would've thrashed the water from the tub when I violently shook with the power of my orgasm. My desire for him was sitting so close to the surface that even the lightest touch would've set me off. And Edge's touch was anything but light.

"Be still," he demanded when I tried to move from his lap. He continued to stroke me slowly, and I could feel yet another orgasm hovering. Just as I was about to explode, Edge pulled his hands away and touched my neck with his lips. "Decker has something he wants to talk to us about."

What? I was on the edge of a mind-blowing orgasm, and he was talking about Decker? "What did you say?" I half moaned, wanting to grab his hand and bring it back to my pussy.

"We'll have to finish this later, little Rebel."

"Wait. What?"

He shifted me off his lap and climbed out, taking my hand to help me stand. Did he expect me to be able to walk?

"Edge?"

"Yes, baby?"

"Do we have to leave?"

"I'm afraid so."

"Right this minute?"

He cupped my cheek after draping a warm towel around my shoulders. "We won't be gone too long."

"But…"

He winked. "Just say it, Rebel."

"I was…I am…"

"Go on."

"So close."

"I see. And you thought I wasn't aware of your current…predicament."

"Well…"

He brought his lips to mine in a chaste kiss. "Don't worry. I'll take care of you, Rebel. Later." He dried me off with the towel, and when he knelt in front of me, I practically thrust myself against his mouth. He looked up into my eyes. "Oh, and Rebel?"

"Yes?" I whined.

"No more orgasms unless it's by my mouth." He kissed the soft spot on the crease of my thigh. "Or my hands. Or my cock. Do you understand?"

I nodded, although I didn't understand. Was he saying I couldn't take my own edge off? I smiled, unable to stop myself from making the connection between his name and the torture he was putting me through.

After he'd rubbed me dry, he helped me get dressed, trailing his fingers over the most sensitive parts of my body and playing it off as an accident each time.

He led me over to the bench at the end of the bed and proceeded to dry off and dress right in front of me, not even trying to hide his erection.

I looked directly at his cock. "You know, I could help you with that."

"I appreciate the offer, little Rebel, but if you have to wait, so do I."

"That's the thing. Neither of us has to wait, Edge."

"But that's what we're going to do."

"Why?"

He held out his hand, I stood, and he pulled me against him. "Because later, when I finish what I've started, the orgasms you'll have will be the best of your life."

Every bump in the road the truck hit registered directly between my legs. In fact, I thought maybe he was maneuvering it in order to drive over as many as possible.

Finally, he pulled into a driveway and cut the engine. The house in front of us was the quintessential farmhouse. It was a two-story with white clapboard and black shutters, and I instantly fell in love with it.

The place Edge lived in was spectacular, but this looked so much like my grandparents' house it almost brought me to tears.

Edge reached over to hold my hand. "Everything okay?"

"I love this house."

He smiled as though he understood.

By the time he came around to open my door, a man had come out and was standing on the porch.

"Rebel, I'd like you to meet Decker." Edge rested his fingers softly on the small of my back. I stepped forward and shook the man's hand.

"Come on in." He motioned for me to walk in front of him.

"Hi," said a woman standing inside the front door. "I'm Mila, Decker's wife. Can I get you anything?"

"A glass of water would be nice, thank you."

Mila disappeared down a hallway while Decker led us to a dining room table.

"It didn't take much digging to come up with something on Possum. The guy made a lot of enemies in his short life."

That didn't surprise me. The man was pure evil.

"Since the list is long, it'll take us a while to sort through who had a motive to want him dead and who might've been at the Long Branch that night."

Decker handed Edge a piece of paper. He skimmed it and raised his eyebrows. "Aryan Brotherhood of Texas?"

"Card-carrying member."

"You didn't know?" I asked, looking between the two of them.

Edge shook his head, but Decker continued as though I hadn't said anything.

"The Bloods and the Mexicales would be at the top of the list of who'd want him dead. Not only Possum, but anyone associated with the ABT."

Edge nodded. "If we're right, with organizations like those, proving who actually killed him would be nearly impossible. However, establishing enough reasonable doubt that Rebel killed him shouldn't be a stretch."

I doubted it would be that easy, and by the look on Edge's face as he spoke, he agreed.

Decker raised his head when Mila walked in with a glass of water.

"I love your house," I told her. I would've had the same smile on my face as she did if it were mine.

"I grew up here. At least part of my childhood."

She looked over at Decker; what passed between them was too private, too personal, and I looked away. The love they had for each other was powerful enough to be felt even without looking. I'd give anything to have a man feel that way about me someday.

My eyes met Edge's when he stood and offered me his hand. "Let's gather the troops and strategize."

Decker walked us out, and while he and Edge didn't speak again, there was plenty I sensed they communicated without words.

10

Edge

Rebel was in more danger than I'd initially realized, which meant I needed to talk both to Mac and Hammer. What stunned and confused me was, if the ABT believed she'd killed one of their own, she would've been dead her first week in jail. Something was off, and the knowledge of Possum's involvement with a white supremacist gang only reinforced my commitment to do everything in my power to keep her safe.

Fortunately, King-Alexander Ranch, given the Alexander family's ties to the intelligence world, had one of the best private security systems I'd ever seen. There were international governments whose security wasn't as sophisticated. As long as she didn't leave without me or one of the other Invincibles by her side, she'd be safe.

As far as the security at the ranch went, I needed to brief Rebel on how it all worked in the event she wanted to take as much as a walk on the property alone. So far, everywhere she'd gone had been with me.

The equipment set up in the house I lived in would allow me to add Rebel to the system. However, doing so might make her feel uncomfortable, given I'd have to scan in her palm and fingers. It would also require facial recognition, which meant she'd have to sit in front of a monitor until it registered her features. The last thing I wanted was for her to feel anything that would remind her of being arrested. Particularly since I knew without any doubt that she wasn't a murderer.

We were almost to the main house when I saw Tee-Tee coming out the front door. I hadn't had a chance to talk to her yet, but I was certain she could use Rebel's help, so I pulled up, cut the engine, and waved at her.

"Hey, Tee-Tee. There's someone I want to introduce you to." By the time I walked around the truck, Rebel had already climbed out and was shooting a glare at me. When I turned around, Tee-Tee had a similar scowl on her face.

"We've already met," muttered Rebel, who stood where she was, next to the truck.

Maybe I'd regret it, but I decided to forge ahead regardless of whatever was going on between the two women.

"Rebel is quite the chef, Tee-Tee. She'll be staying on the ranch for some time, and I thought she might be able to help in the kitchen."

Rebel put her hand on my arm and shook her head when I looked at her. Tee-Tee stood with her arms folded and head cocked.

"We don't have to talk about this right now." I was about to open the truck door when I heard Tee-Tee call out to us.

"Wait," she said, walking closer. When she was within a couple of feet, she looked directly at Rebel. "How are you, Lucy?"

"Fine, *Tía*. How are you?"

"I heard otherwise."

I was about to step in, but stopped when Rebel rested her hand on my arm a second time.

"I didn't kill anyone. I swear on my granddaddy's grave I didn't."

Tee-Tee nodded and took another step closer. "You'd have to be in the kitchen by four for breakfast. You can take a break before and after lunch since not many hands come in, in the middle of the day, but you'll have to be back by three to start dinner."

"It's your decision," I told Rebel when she looked at me.

"I'd like the opportunity."

"Meet me in the dining hall in an hour," Tee-Tee snapped before turning and walking away.

I opened the door and held my hand out to Rebel. She didn't need my help getting in, but I liked that she took it anyway.

As I climbed into the driver's side, my first thought was to ask Decker what he knew about Tee-Tee's relationship with Rebel but decided against it. I'd already asked him to see what he could find out about her mother's death. If I wanted to get to know the beguiling woman sitting beside me, I couldn't continue asking questions behind her back. I needed to learn about Rebel's life directly from her.

"You probably want an explanation," Rebel said as I pulled the truck into the garage.

"An explanation? No."

"Tee-Tee isn't my aunt."

I turned to face her and nodded.

"When I was a teenager, I'd go to her house sometimes. I was friends with her daughter."

"You didn't know she worked here at the ranch?"

Rebel shook her head. "Tee-Tee's daughter, Blanca, and I lost touch."

She didn't make a move to get out of the truck, so I didn't either.

"Blanca…she was pretty messed up."

"Is that why you lost touch?"

"Yeah."

I reached over and took her hand. "I told you before that you don't owe me an explanation. If this is something you don't want to talk about, you don't have to."

Rebel shook her head again. "I want you to hear the truth from me before Tee-Tee tells you." She took a deep breath. "Blanca invited me over one afternoon, and when I got there, she was high on meth. I hated it when she got high, because she'd always try to pick a fight with me. It didn't matter what it was about; I'd learned long before that regardless of what I said, she'd keep arguing. So, I left. I don't think I even said goodbye to Tee-Tee, because I was so mad at Blanca."

I squeezed her fingers. "Go on."

"Early the next morning, Tee-Tee showed up at our house, demanding that my granddaddy get me out of bed. Their arguing woke me up, so I went out to see what was wrong." Rebel took another deep breath.

"She accused me of taking money. A lot of money. I don't remember the amount, but she said she'd had it set aside to pay her rent." Rebel turned her body so she was facing me. "I didn't take it. I swear I didn't."

I brought her hand to my lips. "I believe you."

She scrunched her eyebrows. "Why?"

"I just do."

"You're saying that you, who's known me for a matter of hours, believe me."

"That's right."

"Yet a woman who'd known me most of my life, didn't."

"Did she ever find the money?"

"I don't know."

"What do you think happened to it?"

"I couldn't prove it, but I have no doubt that Blanca took it."

"Did you say so at the time?"

Rebel shook her head. "Not to Tee-Tee. She never would've believed me, and since I didn't have proof, it didn't feel right accusing her. Especially knowing how she'd react."

"What happened after you denied taking the money?"

"She said she was going to press charges against me, but I never heard another word about it."

"What about your granddad? Did he believe you?"

"Yeah, he did. Not long before this happened, he asked why Blanca didn't come around anymore, why I always went to their house. I told him the truth."

"That she was using meth?"

"Yes." After another deep breath, she continued. "My mom was an addict."

"He understood your frustrations with Blanca, then?"

"Yeah. I think he tried to talk to Tee-Tee about it. Not that day, but another time. I don't know for sure, but…that's the kind of man he was."

"Where's Blanca now?"

"Barton Creek Cemetery."

Her blunt answer didn't surprise me, but the fact that Rebel had accepted Tee-Tee's offer to work in the kitchen, did.

"Are you sure about taking the job?"

"I don't have any choice."

"What do you mean?"

"Who else is going to hire me? Let's say that you are able to prove I didn't kill Possum; even then, there are people who are going to doubt it. I may be acquitted, but that doesn't mean someone would take a chance on me. I don't think even Bobby would risk it."

I had so much admiration for the woman sitting next to me. It took a lot of courage for her to set her pride aside the way she did. Something she'd said didn't sit right with me, though.

"We don't have to prove you innocent, Rebel. We need to find who killed him, and make sure they're brought to justice. If we're unable to do that, Hammer will still advocate that there isn't evidence to prove you killed him. Once the court hears who Possum was affiliated with, that alone should be enough for reasonable doubt."

She looked away. "Might as well leave me in jail."

"Why would you say that?"

"Because if you or someone else can't find out who killed him, everyone is going to think I did. They'll think that for the rest of my life."

"Let's take this one step at a time. The first thing you need to do is get ready for work." I got out of the truck and went around to open Rebel's door. When she climbed out, I trapped her between the vehicle and me. "I'm going to kiss you."

"You are?"

I nodded. "Yes. As long as that's okay with you."

She smiled. "I don't know, Edge. As you said, I do need to get ready for work."

"Afraid that once I do, you won't want me to stop?"

"Something like that."

I kissed her long, deep, and hard—the only kind of kiss I could give Rebel. When I took a break and rested my forehead against hers, she ducked under my arm and rushed over to the door. That she couldn't get in reminded me I needed to take care of getting her into the security system before she went to meet Tee-Tee. If it came down to it, I'd call the cook myself to tell her why Rebel was late. The bottom line was, she wouldn't be able to get into the dining hall unless her profile was input.

11

Rebel

I had no idea what to wear. Not that I had a lot of choices. While I appreciated the clothes Shadow had lent me—given me—they weren't at all my style. I wasn't complaining, but for now, jeans and a collared shirt would have to do. If Tee-Tee wanted me to dress another way, she'd let me know. The woman had never been shy about expressing her opinion.

I didn't tell Edge, but when I looked into her eyes earlier, I didn't see anger or judgment or even distrust; I saw warmth. That's the reason I said I wanted the opportunity. It wasn't solely the job. I wanted the opportunity for Tee-Tee and me to be okay again—as much as we could be.

When I walked out of the bedroom and into the kitchen, I didn't see Edge. I still had over a half hour before I needed to be at the dining hall, so I grabbed a glass of water and sat down at the breakfast bar.

As soon as I did, Edge walked out of a door off the kitchen that I hadn't noticed before.

"There you are," he said.

When he leaned in and kissed me, I wondered why I hadn't asked Tee-Tee if I could start tomorrow. It wasn't like I'd forgotten his earlier promise to "take care of me later." How could I? The man had left me on the edge of an orgasm that I knew would be powerful, maybe the most powerful of my life.

"I mentioned earlier that I need to set up your profile in the security system."

I nodded, not knowing what that entailed but sensing some trepidation on Edge's part. He motioned for me to follow him through the same door he'd come out of. When I did, I saw an elaborate computer setup with several monitors.

He pulled out one of the chairs. "Have a seat."

Once I was seated, he set a trackpad by the keyboard. "Put the fingertips of your hand on this." Edge shook his right hand, again like it had fallen asleep.

He flexed his fingers, put his hand on mine, and adjusted the way my fingertips rested. "Hold them like that and look right here. Keep your eyes open." He pointed to the screen. "Okay, you can relax," he said a few seconds later.

"What is this?"

"The system Decker developed uses facial-recognition software for the most part. There are certain areas, though, where the security is more complex, so you'll need to scan your palm and fingertips."

Edge turned the chair and looked into my eyes. "I know this feels intrusive, and I'm sorry for that. However, I can assure you that everyone who sets foot on the ranch has to go through the same process. It's more in-depth if they'll be working here."

I wasn't sure whether I believed him or not. Staring into the computer had felt like having a mug shot taken, and putting my fingers on the trackpad felt like being fingerprinted. It made me feel as much like a criminal today as I had the day I was arrested.

He reached out and cupped my face with his hand. "I wouldn't lie to you, Rebel."

"It feels…the same."

"I know, and I wish it weren't necessary, but it is. If it will make you feel better, ask Tee-Tee about it. She'll tell you the truth in the same way I have. Watch as the ranch hands enter the dining hall; you'll see they go through the same process you will."

I shrugged; until I saw how it worked with my own eyes, I couldn't help but be skeptical.

Edge glanced at his watch. "We should leave."

I followed him out to the garage. He opened the passenger door of the truck, and held out his hand. Instead of helping me in, he drew me into his arms. "Don't think I've forgotten, Rebel. Tonight, you're all mine."

His whispered words sent shivers down my spine. I turned my head, wishing he would kiss me, but he didn't.

"I won't want to stop," he said, as though he'd read my disappointment.

It didn't take long for us to get to the dining hall. Edge pulled up in front, and before he could come around, I jumped out of the truck.

"Don't do that," he muttered when he met me by the front bumper.

"Do what?"

"You're a lady, Rebel, and as such, I expect you to allow me to be a gentleman."

"I can manage—"

"I don't want you to *manage*. The next time you go against my wishes, there will be consequences."

I laughed but he didn't. "You're serious?"

His eyes bored into mine when he nodded.

"What kind of consequences?"

"You'll see."

When he took my hand, my first instinct was to pull away. However, his threat made me think twice. As we approached the main dining hall door, Edge pointed to what looked like a trackpad mounted to the wall. He took my hand and pressed it to the pad. "Look here." He pointed to a screen above it. Within seconds, I heard a click and the door automatically opened.

"If there's ever someone behind you, they'll know not to follow you in. Even if they tried, the door would close before they could get through it."

"This is crazy," I mumbled.

Edge motioned for me to go inside, and as I crossed the threshold, the door closed like he'd predicted it would. I heard another click, the door opened, and Edge joined me.

"Let's find Tee-Tee."

As he said her name, she came out of a set of double doors.

"On time. I was beginning to think you wouldn't be." She motioned me over to her. "You can pick her up after dinner," she said over her shoulder as we walked away.

Edge held up his hand, and I waved goodbye, wishing I had expressed more appreciation for everything he was doing for me.

"I'll give you a tour. After, we'll start prep for dinner."

"If you're too busy, I'm sure someone else could give me a tour."

"I said I'd do it." She motioned again for me to follow.

Twenty minutes later, I had seen the dry-food storage areas, the walk-in coolers, and the main kitchen where the grills and ovens were located. As we walked, she asked me about the different things I liked to cook. Almost everything I told her was a dessert or sweet of some kind.

The last area Tee-Tee showed me was the counter where the food would be set up.

"All the food is served cafeteria-style." She pointed to trash cans set up on the perimeter of the hall. "The hands are expected to clean up after themselves."

We sat at one of the tables, and she explained that the menu was set a week in advance and, rather than having to go out to secure supplies, everything was delivered directly to the kitchen. Each meal was comprised of hearty-yet-fresh-and-healthy food. While

King-Alexander Ranch was self-sustaining in terms of meat and produce, Tee-Tee often traded with other ranches for specialty items. That way, the cowboys and ranch hands weren't served the same meals again and again.

On the menu for tonight was Texas-style chili, a spinach salad, cornbread, and dessert.

"What's the dessert?" I asked when Tee-Tee didn't elaborate.

"That's up to you to figure out," she answered before walking away.

"Wait! What do you mean?"

Tee-Tee looked over her shoulder. "You know where everything is stored. Go see what's there. After you've made your decision about what you'll make, come back and tell me."

"You've got to be kidding," I mumbled, not thinking she'd hear me, but she did.

"You can do it."

Those four words brought tears to my eyes. I'd been estranged from Tee-Tee for so long, never dreaming we'd ever reconcile, let alone that she'd have faith in me. The fact that she did and admitted it, surprised me as much as it made me emotional.

In the dry storage rooms, I found baking flour, sugar, and the other ingredients I'd need to make a basic cake. Since I remembered seeing oranges and clementines in the coolers, along with buttermilk and eggs, it only took me ten minutes to come up with my decision. When I walked into the kitchen, Tee-Tee was standing with her back to one of the prep tables. She raised her eyebrows.

"Orange-scented buttermilk cakes with a simple vanilla drizzle and topped with slices of clementines."

She didn't respond, but I caught the hint of her smile and knew she was pleased.

"Thank you for giving me this opportunity, *Tía*. I know—"

She held up her hand. "Don't make me regret it."

"I won't. I promise."

With dessert being my only responsibility for this evening's meal, I learned how to operate the big industrial-size mixers along with the massive ovens. I also learned that Tee-Tee had developed an easy system for multiplying any recipe in order to feed the number of workers on the ranch at any given time. Since December was a slow time of the year on any operation like this one, I was shocked by the number of people expected tonight.

"Quint Alexander and Decker Ashford don't believe in a seasonal crew," Tee-Tee explained.

"They don't?" The idea of it shocked me, not that I understood the intricate details of running an operation of this size.

She didn't elaborate, and I didn't ask any questions that didn't relate solely to making my dessert.

As I took the last sheet out of the oven, I heard the dinner bell ring. All I had left to do was drizzle the icing and lay the slices of fruit on top of each cake, but in order to have it ready when the diners were, I had to stay focused on my task. I was so involved I didn't notice when Tee-Tee approached and stood next to me until she cleared her throat.

"Is everything all right?" I asked, worried that I'd done something wrong.

"Look." She motioned with her head.

I smiled when I saw Edge dishing up a big bowl of chili before grabbing two pieces of cornbread. Just when I thought he'd walk away without noticing me, he looked into my eyes and winked.

"Es un buen hombre," I heard Tee-Tee say. *"Trátalo bien."*

I agreed. Edge was a good man, and he deserved to be treated well. "I will, *Tía*, I promise."

12

Edge

Knowing Rebel would be working through the end of dinner gave me time to get some work done. The first thing I did was make sure my partners were on board with us taking this on as a job.

"I'll be covering the costs for this one," I told them when we gathered at the ranch's main house. "Rebel was released into my custody."

In response, three of the four men seated at the table shook their heads.

Deck was the first to speak. "Out of the question."

I'd expected that reaction from him. The first job we'd done after the Invincibles formed was essentially asset protection for the woman who was now Decker's wife. It had turned into a great deal more, but even then, I wouldn't have taken a dime in payment from Decker; Rile and Grinder felt the same.

I turned to the fourth man at the table, my brother. He hadn't officially signed on with our firm, but even if he had, I wouldn't have let him work this job.

"Come with me." I led Lennox out to the front porch.

"I can help with this," he said before the door shut behind us.

"I won't allow it."

"It isn't your decision."

My older brother became my guardian when our parents died, and he still attempted to exercise a role of authority with me. However, I'd stopped standing for it years ago.

"You haven't officially joined the Invincibles, Lennox. Therefore, it is my decision, and I intend to enforce it. Besides, you've already said you're leaving in the morning."

He sat down on a chair and looked out at the rolling hills. "Going to Boston may prove a waste of time."

"It may, but it could also be the best decision you make in your life." During the mission in which I was shot, my brother had met and fallen in love with a woman who lived on the East Coast. Her name was Emerson and they'd actually met years ago. Because of me, he'd been separated from her for over three months. If I'd realized that he hadn't communicated with her that entire time, I would've tossed my brother out of the rehab hospital on his ear.

"Right."

When I went inside, Lennox didn't follow, and I was glad of it. He had his own problems to work out.

With that settled, at least in my mind, I placed a call to Hammer, asking him to join us at the ranch. While we worked to figure out who'd killed Possum, I needed him to do whatever he could on the legal side to get the charges against Rebel dropped. I considered inviting the sheriff to join us, but fearing a conflict of interest that might compromise Rebel's release on bail, I decided against it. Tomorrow, without Hammer present, I'd arrange to meet with Mac.

"Got a minute?" asked Grinder when I walked back inside.

"Of course."

He led me over to the dining room table, and we both sat down.

"Talk to me about this woman. You're arse over elbows."

Grinder was my best friend in the world, so it made sense that he'd be the first to notice how out of character my behavior was—even before my brother.

"I met her before we left on the last mission."

My friend nodded. "And?"

I told him everything that had happened, including that initially, I'd been certain I was the one who'd killed the tosser.

"When Hammer negotiated bail, I volunteered for custody."

"Do you think she did it?"

I shook my head. "I know she didn't." I explained Decker had told me an hour ago that he and Mac had uncovered Possum's involvement with the Aryan Brotherhood.

"Could've been a hit."

I agreed. Not only could have been, more than likely, that's exactly what it was.

"What do you see happening?"

"I sent a message to Hammer, asking him to meet me here. I was hoping I could get Decker here too, so we can put together an action plan."

"Understood, but first, what do you see happening with this woman?" He unnecessarily emphasized the last two words. My answer had been an intentional attempt to circumvent his real question.

It took me a long time to answer, and Grinder, pain in the arse that he could be, waited patiently.

"I don't know."

He shook his head. "Not good, mate."

Three words on each of our parts, and yet they communicated so much. If Rebel hadn't worked her way under my skin, I would've told Grinder that once she was exonerated, we'd part ways. I wouldn't have hesitated either. His response was right on the money too. If I didn't know, that meant I was in over my head.

"She doesn't have anyone else who can help her."

Grinder nodded. "So you're the white knight."

Truthfully, I'd been the black knight far more often in my life. I couldn't treat Rebel the same way I'd treated other women—walking away when I was done shagging them. For the time being anyway, she was living in my house.

"I arranged for her to work in the dining hall with Tee-Tee." I also told Grinder that they already knew each other but left out the details of their estrangement.

"Begs the question whether you plan to stay in the States long term?"

It wasn't that I didn't love England. However, the argument could be made that even before I spent time here, I preferred the idea of the States, Texas in particular, over my motherland. Would I have felt differently if my parents hadn't died when I was a lad? It was impossible to say since they had.

I'd never made a secret of my desire to stay on here as long as possible. It was something Grinder and Rile regularly gave me shit about. Even Lennox enjoyed taking the piss out of me from time to time. In his case, it was my fascination with the cowboy lifestyle that he enjoyed poking fun at.

Before I could respond to Grinder's question, which I assumed to be rhetorical anyway, Rile and Decker walked in.

"We need to come up with a better place to meet," Grinder said, noticing Shadow first walk in and then out again. "And somewhere else to stay."

"Agreed." Rile brushed his index finger over his lips. The two had been staying at the ranch's main house, both thinking they'd only be here a short time.

Quint walked in and sat at the table. "There are other houses on the ranch that no one is living in." He looked at me. "Not as nice as the one you're in."

"It isn't necessary that you house our crew," said Rile. "We aren't with SIS any longer."

Given that Quint's father was the chief of MI6, when we all worked under him, we'd stayed at the ranch when missions brought us to this part of the States. The place provided the type of security we'd needed to execute our ops. Rile was right. Now that we were an independent entity, we couldn't continue relying on Quint's hospitality.

I hated the idea I'd need to find another place to live. However, the bottom line was, the level of international intelligence work we did, didn't leave time for me to simultaneously live out my childhood dream of being a ranch hand. Quint shouldn't be supplying housing for me any more than for Grinder or Rile.

"It's foolish for you to stay anywhere else." Quint set the salt shaker in front of him and moved the pepper shaker to the side. "Here's where we are." He picked up the salt and set it down. "Here's where Edge is." He did the same thing with the pepper. He'd run out of seasoning to illustrate his point, so he used his finger. "There's a house here, here, and here. All sitting vacant. I doubt any of you will stick around Texas after you've worked this job." Quint looked at me again. "For lack of a better word."

I nodded. "Job is as good a word as any."

"Stay on the ranch for the time being. It's no skin off my back." He smiled at Shadow, who was standing in the kitchen, listening to our conversation. "I'll admit it will be nice to have the main house to ourselves."

"Can we get down to business now?" asked Decker.

When we all muttered our agreement, he continued. "We need to get someone on the inside of the Aryan Brotherhood."

I agreed.

"What about Ink?" asked Grinder.

Both Rile and I shook our heads. I doubted he was thinking the same thing I was, but maybe.

"Jagger?"

Rile was back to stroking his finger over his lip. "I'm thinking a different approach would be best."

"Me," I blurted. All eyes turned to me, except for Rile's.

Grinder opened his mouth, but before he could speak, Rile held up his hand. "Casper will go in with him."

The woman was as badass as they came. A job this size would take two agents. It made far more sense that she and I go in as a couple than it would for another bloke to go in with me.

Rile turned to Grinder. "Please get her and Ink here as quickly as possible. I'll see if the agency still has someone inside the Aryan Nation."

"What are we bringing Ink in for?" I asked.

"Ms. Marks is in your custody. Have you forgotten?"

I hadn't, but I wouldn't necessarily choose Ink to take over for me. But who instead? Rile, Grinder, and Deck would have their hands full, monitoring the ABT while Casper and I were inside.

After I nodded at Grinder, he turned to Rile. "Roger that."

Rile stood. "We'll regroup in the morning."

"At whichever house you stick me with," Grinder said before he and I walked out.

"By the way," I said once we were out of earshot, "the house closest to the one I'm living in is the nicest."

"Tell Rile that I'll take that one." He smiled and patted me on the back before he walked away.

I checked my mobile, wondering why I hadn't gotten a return message from Hammer. When I tapped the screen, I saw a missed call instead. It was odd that I didn't get an alert.

He didn't answer when I rang back, so I sent another text rather than leave a voicemail.

Noticing Lennox's rental was still parked out front, I looked around for my brother, but didn't see him. A few seconds later, he came out of the barn.

"Boon yakked you up?" The barn manager was known for striking up conversations that could go on for hours.

Lennox nodded. "I made the mistake of walking over to the corral."

I laughed and put my hand on my brother's shoulder. "Tell me you're leaving in the morning."

"I am."

"I'm happy to hear it. You and Emerson are meant for each other." I'd known it the first time I saw them together, which was also the first time I met her. I sincerely hoped they were able to work things out, particularly since I felt guilty that he'd spent so much time with me during my recovery.

"I've booked a room at a hotel near the airport. My flight leaves quite early."

"Godspeed, Lennox."

"Godspeed, Keon."

It was something we always said whenever we were together and one or both of us were leaving. It began shortly after our parents died.

As I watched my brother walk away, I heard the dinner bell ring, and my stomach grumbled. I hadn't had anything to eat since I grabbed one of Rebel's cinnamon rolls this morning, and I was famished. Instead of heading back to the house where there was little food I could turn into something worth eating, I walked over to the dining hall.

The minute I walked inside, I knew that Tee-Tee was serving Texas chili and cornbread. It was one of my favorite meals. Thankfully, there weren't many in line in front of me since I was ready to chew my arm off from the scents alone. I approached the counter and saw Rebel concentrating on whatever she was making. It looked like a cake of some kind.

I let the guy standing behind me go ahead so I could continue watching her unnoticed. If Rebel had been born into a different life, the woman could've been a supermodel. Her features were exquisite, and her body was smashingly lush. She said she'd noticed me at the Long Branch, but I didn't remember seeing her before the night we met. Looking at her now, I had no idea how I could've missed her.

By watching her, I was making myself as randy as I was hungry. As I grabbed two pieces of cornbread after dishing up my chili, Rebel looked up and her eyes met mine. My first instinct was to smile and wink. When she smiled too, I wanted to jump the counter and take her in my arms. Why was my physical reaction to this woman so intense?

I noticed Tee-Tee standing next to her, and the pride that shone on her face warmed my heart. I shook my head at my reaction. Damn good thing none of my mates were with me or I'd never hear the end of it. Grinder in particular. As he'd said, I was arse over elbows for this woman.

Rebel went back to what she was doing, and I went in search of an open seat. I was one of the first to arrive, so there were many to choose from. As I typically did, I sat in the back corner of the room, in a chair that faced in.

"Why do you always sit back here?" Tee-Tee asked when she walked up to me a few minutes later.

"No surprises," I told her as I raised my head and scanned the room like I'd done every few seconds while I ate.

"She did well today."

"You don't need to report to me, Tee-Tee. In fact, I'd prefer if you didn't."

She pulled out the chair next to me and sat down. "Did she tell you what happened?"

"Between the two of you? Yes."

I studied her as she looked off into the distance.

"Do you still believe she stole from you?"

Tee-Tee took a deep breath and let it out slowly. "No."

"Does Rebel know that?"

She looked at me. "You care about her."

"She's alone in this world."

"It's more than that," she said, resting her hand on my arm. "Isn't it?"

"Maybe. I'm not sure how to define the way I feel."

"Does Rebel know that?" she asked with a wink.

I winked back. "I'd appreciate it if you kept mum on the subject."

She smiled, stood, and walked away. A few minutes later, Rebel came out of the kitchen carrying two plates.

"What's this?" I asked when she got closer.

"Dessert. Tee-Tee told me to bring you some; she suggested I have some too."

When she set the plate in front of me, more than wanting it, I wanted her. If we were alone, I'd pull her onto my lap and feast on the soft skin on her neck.

"Tell me if you like it."

I noticed her hands folded so tightly her knuckles were white. "I can already tell you I do."

"Taste it anyway."

I brought the fork to my mouth, and the sweet cake melted on my tongue. "Oh my God," I groaned. "This is brilliant."

"Do you really like it?"

I nodded as I shoved another helping into my mouth, immediately followed by a third. "Is there more?"

When Rebel's cheeks turned bright pink and she lowered her eyes, I was back to wanting to pull her onto my lap.

"Look at me," I demanded.

Startled, she did.

"It's fantastic. Is this your recipe?"

"How did you know?"

"If it were Tee-Tee's and she'd made it before, it would be the most requested dessert the ranch hands ever had."

"Seriously?"

I nodded as I shoved two more forkfuls into my mouth. I hoped she wouldn't swat my hand when I ate hers as well. "What is it?"

"A simple orange cake."

I shook my head. "There is nothing simple about this. What's the secret ingredient?"

She laughed. "There isn't one."

"Sure there is, and I've figured out what."

She cocked her head. "You have?"

I nodded. "You made it."

13

Rebel

This man wasn't only hot as fuck, he was sweet too. A lethal combination for me. There was no way I could allow myself to get used to being around him or to the life I'd been thrust into.

Tee-Tee was sweet to give me this opportunity, but it wasn't permanent. As I reminded myself often, I was in Edge's custody. I wasn't his guest or his live-in girl-friend. We weren't even lovers, not yet.

"What are you thinking about?"

"Nothing," I answered, noticing he'd stopped eating.

"Don't do that."

"What do you mean?"

"Don't keep things from me."

This wasn't the first time Edge's quick transition from playful to serious startled me. One minute he was smiling, and the next he looked like he wanted to take me over his knee and spank me. "I'm not keeping things from you."

He grabbed the chair and turned it, with me in it, so I was facing him. Something told me that if I lied, he'd know it.

"I was thinking how nice this was. You, Tee-Tee…"

"And?"

When I shook my head, he scrunched his eyes. I bit my bottom lip, wishing he wouldn't persist. "It'll end." I willed my eyes not to fill with tears. I hated self-pity.

"Why does it have to end?"

"Once this is…over and I'm not staying here anymore, I doubt that Tee-Tee will still let me work here."

He motioned toward the kitchen with his head. "You sure about that?"

All of the dessert plates were gone, and I'd put out far more servings than there were people here. "Wow," I mumbled.

"Wow is right. That takes care of your doubt that Tee-Tee will keep you on. Now let's discuss the rest."

"What rest?"

Edge leaned in closer to me and grasped my chin with his hand. "Don't play dumb with me, little Rebel. I know you're not. I'll prompt you. Once this is over and you're not staying here anymore…"

I tried to scoot back, but Edge's other hand kept the chair where it was. "What is there to discuss? One way or another, this will be over. Either I'll be back in jail, or someone will figure out who really killed Possum."

"I've already told you that you're not going back to jail. Tell me what you see happening once I figure out who killed him."

Why was he pushing me so hard? I jerked the chair away, stood, and stalked back to the kitchen, knowing damn well he wouldn't make a scene in the dining hall.

I was about to walk into the employee restroom when I felt Tee-Tee's hand on my arm. "What happened, *Mija*?"

"Please, don't," I said, pulling away from her and rushing into the bathroom. I rested my back against the door after I'd closed and locked it.

What was it with these two? Yesterday, Tee-Tee wouldn't have given me the time of day if we'd passed on the street. Today she was calling me her daughter. And Edge—what the hell was his problem? The minute this thing with Possum was over, we would be too. What kind of sadist was he that he wanted me to say it out loud?

"Rebel, open the door," I heard him say from the other side of it.

I moved closer to the stalls. "Go away."

"You have until the count of three to open this bloody door. If you don't, I'm coming in anyway. One…two…"

I rushed over and threw the lock. I'd get fired for sure if Edge broke the bathroom door open on my first day because of me. I backed away when he came inside and locked it behind him.

"I'm sorry."

I raised my head. That was the last thing I expected him to say.

"I overreacted, and I wish I could explain why."

I looked into his eyes. "I wish you could too."

"You said this will end, and I don't want it to. I know how fucked up that sounds. I want this thing with Possum to go away. I want you exonerated as soon as possible. What I don't want is for you to think the minute that happens, I'll want you to leave."

I was dumbfounded. "Edge…"

He took two steps toward me. "What, Rebel?"

"I'm not an idiot."

"I think I already covered that when I told you not to play dumb with me."

"This isn't funny."

"I agree. Now get back to what you were going to say."

"I'm in your custody."

"That's merely a formality. You're here because I want you to be."

I couldn't look at him when I said what I was about to say, so I turned my back. "You are way out of my league."

I didn't hear him walk closer, but his arm was suddenly around my waist, spinning me around to face him. "That's bullshit."

I tried to move away, but this time, his grasp on me was firm. "Until everything went down with Possum, you didn't know I existed."

"How is that relevant?"

"If I weren't out of your league, you would've noticed me."

His eyes softened, which made my urge to bolt stronger.

"Don't you dare feel sorry for me." More than self-pity, I hated it from anyone else. "You don't know a thing about me and vice versa."

He moved his hand to the back of my neck and leaned closer. "I want to know you." Before I could respond, he kissed me. And, of course, my traitorous body fell right into line.

Edge rested his forehead against mine. "What do you say we vacate the lavatory in case someone else needs it?"

As much as I was all for getting out of here, I didn't want to face the kitchen staff. Tee-Tee especially. "I feel like such an idiot."

Edge shook his head. "Don't talk about yourself like that. I don't like it."

This time when I pulled away, he let me. "You're kind of weird, Edge. You know that?" I walked out, hoping he wouldn't grab me and tell me he didn't like it when I said bad things about him either.

Instead of a bunch of people staring at me, the kitchen was empty. It looked like it had been cleaned up too.

"It was a good first day," said Tee-Tee, coming around the corner. "Don't forget, we start at five tomorrow morning."

"You said four."

"I wanted to see if you were serious." She turned off the lights and walked out.

Before my eyes adjusted to the darkness, I felt Edge's arm around my waist.

"Let's go."

"How can you see where you're going?"

"I have night vision."

"You do?"

"Hell, no."

Tee-Tee, or someone else, turned a light on near the front door, making it possible for us to see our way out.

With every step I took toward the truck, I felt more tired. Was it only yesterday that I got out of jail? It seemed more like a week.

"As soon as we're back at the house, I'll draw you a bath," Edge said as I climbed in the passenger seat, too exhausted to argue.

14

Edge

By the time I came out of the lavatory, Rebel was fast asleep on my bed. She hadn't even removed her boots. As much as I didn't want to wake her, I knew she couldn't be comfortable. As gently as I could, I loosened the laces and slid each boot off her feet. Next, I eased off her socks.

She rolled to her side but didn't wake, so I lay down behind her and wrapped my arm around her waist. Feeling her next to me was enough for now. Even my cock played along by not wanting to be a part of the action that wouldn't be taking place tonight.

When my phone vibrated, I grabbed it from my pocket, certain Rebel would wake up, but she didn't. I rolled off the bed and crept out of the room. By then, Grinder had hung up, but I rang him straight back.

"Heard I missed a good dessert tonight."

"That bloody well better not be why you rang."

He laughed. "I wanted you to know that Casper and Kick are on their way."

"I hope they know to come in dark. Wait a minute. Did you say Kick? What happened to Ink?"

"Unavailable."

"Who the hell is Kick?"

"Someone Rile has been trying to recruit."

"From where?"

"My guess is the agency."

I got a bad feeling in the pit of my stomach. I didn't like the fact that Rile had made a change without consulting me first. It was something I intended to address when we met later. "Have you ever run an op with him?"

"Negative."

"Where's Ink anyway?" I asked.

"Somewhere in South America. By the way, doesn't that house have any draperies?"

"Where are you?"

"Next door."

"Why do I need window coverings?"

"Because I don't want to look out my window and see you starkers. Wouldn't mind seeing Rebel, though."

"Sod off," I said before ending the call. I didn't give a shit who saw me naked, but I drew the line at who saw her. As far as I was concerned, no one would but me.

"Edge?" I heard her sweet voice say.

"I'm here," I answered, walking back to the bedroom.

"I must have fallen asleep. I'm sorry."

"Don't be. You're exhausted."

"But you were filling the bathtub."

I put my arm around her neck, drew her close to me, and kissed the side of her face. "It's likely cold by now."

"I'm sorry," she repeated.

I lifted her into my arms and carried her back to the bed I wished I could share with her. Soon I would, but not tonight. I set her on her feet and pulled back the bedclothes. "In, you go."

"I should change."

"Right." How had it slipped my mind she was still wearing the clothes she'd been in all day? Probably because I didn't dare imagine her without them. "I'll step out."

I was almost to the bedroom door when I felt her hand on my shoulder. "Edge, did I do something wrong?"

I turned around and scrubbed my face with my hand. "Of course you didn't. I'm trying to be a…God, it sounds so ridiculous, but I'm trying to be a gentleman."

"Why?"

The earnestness of her question made me smile. "Because I thought that's what I should do. You had a long day, sweetness, and an early morning tomorrow."

"Even if you don't want to, you know, do anything, would you mind lying next to me?"

"I would like nothing more." Should I tell her that I'd already done so?

"It felt so good to have you next to me earlier."

I was certain my cheeks flushed like hers often did. "I thought you were asleep."

"I knew you were there."

Rebel smiled in that way that nearly sent me off my trolley. I wanted this woman more than any other, yet I was the one hesitating. She stood close enough to touch, so I did. I cupped her cheek with my palm and stared into her eyes. "Would you like me to warm the bath?"

"Maybe a shower would be better. I might fall asleep in the tub."

I nodded, took her hand, and led her back to the bed. "Take off the rest of your clothes while I get things ready."

"Wait," she said when I tried to release her hand. "Will you join me?"

I couldn't explain how conflicted I felt, even to myself. I wanted to fuck her enough to throw her onto the bed, rip her clothes from her body, and thrust my raging cock into her wetness. Yet, I didn't. Or was it that I couldn't? For maybe the first time in my life, my brain was doing the thinking rather than any other part of my anatomy.

Rebel would give her body to me willingly. She had, in fact. But I wanted more. I wanted to be the man who put her first. She was dead-on-her-feet tired, and tomorrow she'd have to be back at the dining hall before dawn.

"Never mind." She tried to pull away, but this time, I held her hand more tightly.

"I want you, little Rebel. Make no mistake about that. But if we do this tonight, I won't want to let you sleep. I'll want your body in every way I imagined taking it. I'll wring you out and then take even more, because I know, without a shadow of a doubt, that I'll never get enough of you."

She took a deep breath and let it out slowly as I brought my lips to hers. "Let me take care of you another way, sweetness."

Of everything I said, or didn't say, those words appeared to affect her more than any other. Her eyes filled with tears, and she tried to turn away, but I wasn't having it. I didn't only want her body, I wanted her words, her feelings, I wanted it all—I wanted her soul.

I held her face with my hand and forced her to look into my eyes. "Tell me why that made you cry."

"It's been a long time…"

"Go on. Tell me."

"This is hard."

"Do it anyway."

"It's been a long time since anyone has taken care of me." When she leaned forward and buried her face in my shoulder, I let her. I could feel the wetness of her tears.

"Then, let me."

"I don't know how."

"I'll show you." Even though we were standing next to it, I picked her up like I had a few minutes ago and set her on the bed. I removed her clothes as gently as I had taken off her boots and socks when she was sleeping. "Wait here," I said, grabbing the throw from the end of the bed and wrapping it around her shoulders.

Rather than start the shower, I refilled the bath. If she fell asleep, like she predicted she might, I'd be there to hold her. I took off my clothes, wrapped a towel around my waist, and went back into the bedroom.

This time she hadn't fallen asleep; she was far too emotional to let herself. I understood that. Before I did anything else, I had to reassure her but in a way that also let her know that tonight wouldn't be about fucking.

I kissed her forehead, eyelids, and lips before I picked her up again and carried her to the bath.

"I can walk. I'm not that tired."

"I want to feel you in my arms." I rested her on the edge, checked the water, and helped her in.

"You're something, Edge. It's a wonder that there aren't women lined up at the gate, begging for more after treatment like this." She didn't look at me when she said it, which only reinforced the idea that she was putting up walls to keep me at a distance where she felt comfortable. My guess was that she used sex in the same way. Sex, she could control. Emotion, she couldn't.

Without responding, I eased into the water and sat behind her. In the same way I had earlier, I poured body wash into my hand and rubbed it into her shoulders.

Within seconds, her head fell forward as she allowed herself to enjoy letting me ease her tired muscles.

I continued washing every part of her body, but chastely. There were times I sensed she was about to say something, perhaps like the quip she had earlier, but each time, I shushed her.

When I finished, I lifted her limp body from the water, dried her with a warm towel, and carried her to the bed, thankful that she didn't protest with every step.

"I'll be right back," I told her, pulling the bedclothes over her naked body.

After drying myself, I got into bed behind her and pulled her as close to me as I could get her.

"What you said earlier, Rebel, about my treating other women the way I'm treating you tonight, I haven't. Not ever."

"Edge…"

"It's the truth. One thing I'll never do is lie to you."

15

Rebel

I wanted to believe him, but I couldn't. Deep down, I knew Edge was too good to be true, or maybe it was that I knew in my heart that he was too good for me. Guys like him wanted me in their bed…until they didn't, and by that time, I was long gone anyway.

Maybe that's why he was holding off. In fact, it was the only thing that made sense. He knew as well as I did that once he "wrung me out," he actually would have had enough of me. And then what?

After I'd told him I had nothing, it must have dawned on him that what he'd signed up for was way beyond what he initially thought.

When he took his arm from around my waist, I expected him to ease out of the bed and tiptoe out of the room. Instead, he brought it to my shoulder.

"The bath was supposed to relax you, Rebel. You're getting more tense by the second."

"I'm fine," I mumbled, not knowing what else to say.

When he moved my hair over my shoulder, I could feel his warm breath against my neck.

"Let me ask you a question."

"Okay."

"Was your grandfather a good man?"

I took a deep breath, hoping my voice wouldn't betray the emotion that came along with that question. "The best."

"Then you know they do exist."

I didn't remember falling asleep, but what felt like five minutes later, Edge was rubbing my shoulder and telling me it was time to get up.

"What time is it?" I groaned.

"Half past three."

"I don't have to be there until five."

"Consider this your half-hour warning, then. Go back to sleep, sweetness."

When he kissed my cheek and snuggled me against him, I could feel his hardness nestled against the cheeks of my bottom. Given the things he'd said last night, I stopped myself from suggesting we could fill the time with something other than sleep.

I was done being rejected by him. If Edge wanted to have sex with me, he would have to say so. More than say so, he'd have to be the one to act on it. For fun, I wiggled my butt; I had no intention of making it easy for him, though.

"Be careful, little Rebel."

"Or what?"

"I warned you before that there are consequences to bad behavior."

"Maybe you shouldn't be sleeping with your body plastered against mine."

Much to my disappointment, he smoothed my hair and murmured for me to go back to sleep.

When four fifteen rolled around, I was still wide awake. I slipped out of the other side of the bed, grabbed the clothes I'd planned to wear today, and tip-toed into the hallway to use the other bathroom. I don't know why I thought it would be quieter than the one in the master; I blamed my still-sleepy brain.

From there, I went to the kitchen to start a pot of coffee. While I sat and waited for it to brew, it dawned on me that I'd have to wake Edge to take me to the dining hall. Once I had a few sips of hot coffee, it also dawned on me that he'd said we'd do something about Susan yesterday, and we didn't.

I did remember him saying she probably had a dead battery. Likely, he didn't want to spend the money to buy a new one. I could understand that. Later today, I'd try to figure out how to ask Tee-Tee if I would be getting paid or if I'd been given the job at the dining hall in order to earn my keep.

I put my face in my hands. I hated being so dependent on another person. While I hadn't made a lot of money at the bar or the diner, what I made was mine. I'd used it to rent an apartment. It was crappy, but like the money, it was mine. When I removed my hands to take another drink of coffee, Edge was standing right in front of me.

"Jesus," I screeched. "You scared the crap out of me."

"Sorry. I'm used to moving about quietly."

"Why? Do you get some kind of perverse pleasure out of startling people?"

He smiled. "It has more to do with what I do for a living, and I can assure you, there's no pleasure in it, perverse or otherwise."

"Why do you do it?"

He walked over to the coffeemaker, poured a cup, and took a sip. "God, woman, even your coffee is amazing."

I smiled. "Thanks, but you didn't answer my question."

"You and Grinder would get on well." He shook his head. "Forget I said that."

I drummed my fingers on the counter.

"Right. Well, I do it because there are a lot of evil people in the world."

"And you see it as your duty to rid the world of them?"

"Something like that."

"Sorry you had to get up so early."

"Early?" he asked, looking at his cell phone.

Like with my car, it annoyed the piss out of me that I didn't have one. I rested my chin on my hand. This was my life now, and I better damn well get used to it. The idea that I'd ever make money again, let alone enough to fix my car or pay for a phone, was laughable.

"I'd give a hundred pounds to know what you're thinking."

"If you mean that, I'll tell you." I shook my head. "Just kidding."

I swear I barely blinked and he was standing right in front of me again. He reached out and grasped the back of my neck. "Tell me."

"I was kidding. *God.*"

"If that's true, tell me."

Now he was pissing me off. "I need to go to work. If that's what it is."

"What does that mean?"

"No one mentioned an hourly rate. I assumed that maybe I was working off my debt."

Edge took a step back. "What debt?"

I waved my arm. "Staying here." I lifted my cup of coffee. "Food." I set the cup back down. "Let's see, what else? Oh, yeah, one hundred thousand dollars bail?"

"Let's go."

Evidently, I struck a nerve. I jumped off the barstool, followed him out to the garage, and stopped dead in my tracks.

"When…I mean…how?" There, next to the old Ford truck, sat Susan. Not only was she there, but she was clean.

"You didn't exactly keep the place you hid your key a secret."

"When did you do this?"

"To be honest, I had someone else do it."

"Well…thank you. I'd ask what I owe you, but maybe you should add it to my tab."

Edge spun around. "Stop that."

I turned around to see if there was a clock anywhere, but there wasn't one. "Sorry, but what time is it?"

"We need to go."

"We?"

"Get in the truck."

"But my car is here."

"I don't want you driving it until I've had it checked out."

I put my hands on my hips. "For what?"

"To make sure it's safe."

"I guess it was safe enough for whoever you had drive it here."

"It was towed."

"Oh." So much for me thinking I might have a small amount of independence. It probably still needed a battery.

I stalked over to the truck, and before I could open the door, Edge's hand covered mine. "I told you not to do that either," he growled.

I stared him down. "For God's sake. I'm capable of opening a door, Edge. I'm also capable of having thoughts I don't want to share with anyone."

What did he do? He kissed me. *Kissed me!* What the fuck? "Why did you do that?"

"Because you are fucking hot when you're angry. Now get in the truck. You don't want to be late for your job. The one you're getting paid to do."

I refused to look at him as we drove to the dining hall. When he pulled up, the truck wasn't even in park before I opened the door, jumped out, and stomped off. As I was learning to expect, Edge got to the dining hall first and blocked my way.

"Don't say I didn't warn you."

"What does that mean?"

He wrapped his arm around my waist. "We'll deal with your consequences later. Have a good morning at work, darling."

I turned my head when he leaned forward to kiss me.

"And the list continues to grow. I'm going to enjoy this."

"Enjoy what?"

"You'll see." He stepped out of my way, waved his hand, and walked back to the truck.

I was about to put my hand on the pad by the door when I heard him yell, "Rebel, hold up!"

Exasperated, I spun around. "What now?"

"My number as well as Tee-Tee's, Shadow's, and Grinder's are already programmed in," he said, handing me a cell phone. "But don't call him unless it's an emergency."

16

Edge

I checked my mobile as soon as I got back in the truck, brassed the hell off that I still hadn't heard back from Hammer. It was too early for me to ring him again, so I drove over to the barn. I was too late to make the morning chore ride out, but I could check the board and try to catch up.

I walked into the barn manager's office. "Mornin', Boon."

"Jesus, you sound more like a Yank every day, Edge. Might even be pickin' up a Texas accent."

"Ah, don't say it if you don't mean it, Boon," I fired back with an exaggerated drawl.

"You're late."

"Yeah. Sorry. Had to give my girl a ride to work."

"Heard somethin' about that."

"Yeah? From whom?"

Boon raised his eyebrows as though I'd insulted him by suggesting he didn't know everything that happened on the ranch—sometimes even before it happened.

"Tee-Tee told you, didn't she?" I'd been teasing, but the look on his face told me I'd hit on something.

"The crew is headed up to Schoolhouse if you want to be of any help this morning."

"Thanks, Boon." I'd have time to tease him about Tee-Tee later. Morning chores didn't wait.

Schoolhouse was a pasture I was familiar with, and not in a good way. Over a year ago, I'd ridden out with Quint and a couple of the other cowboys when we were ambushed by a gang out to kidnap someone who was at the ranch under MI6 protection.

Not only had the way I rode from that day on changed, the already over-the-top security system got even more complex. Turned out it wasn't as compromised as it had appeared that night. As we later learned, Decker had it programmed in such a way that even if it was disarmed, there were drones and cameras all over the ranch, recording every move made. Less than two hours after the ambush, all ten of the bastards who thought they'd gotten the better of us were stone-cold dead. I couldn't help but smile. That had been a damn good night. Nothing I liked better than putting evildoers down. Well, almost nothing. I liked shagging a whole hell of a lot better.

Thinking about shagging made me think about Rebel. If she thought I was joking earlier, she was in for a big surprise. I'd warned her about consequences, and I intended to deliver on my word. Stopping myself from fucking her after that would be the ultimate test of my control—one I didn't intend to fail. I'd just make that the last of the consequences.

The hair on the back of my neck stood on end when I heard the sound of someone on horseback headed my way. I spun my horse around and drew my gun, only to put it back when I saw it was Grinder approaching.

"Tried to catch you before you left the barn."

"What's up?"

He rode up next to me. "We need to talk, mate."

"Get on with it, then."

"I found something in Rebel's car last night."

I motioned for him to continue.

"A gun. Same caliber as what killed Possum."

"Jesus fucking Christ."

"Sorry, Edge."

"Where?"

"In the boot and not very bloody well hidden."

"Where in the boot, Grind?"

"Under the torn carpet."

"You're certain?"

"Quite."

I breathed a sigh of relief. Albeit temporary.

"What of it?" he asked.

"It wasn't there two nights ago."

"You're certain?" he repeated my words.

"Quite. Someone planted it between then and now, which means that someone was watching us." Something else occurred to me. "Have it swept."

"Understood."

When my friend rounded his horse and took off, I was right behind him.

Decker took care of having Rebel's car swept for devices of any kind while Grinder and I waited at his new place for Rile to arrive with Casper and Kick.

Calla "Casper" Rey and I had worked together on a number of ops both for SIS and privately. She liked to say she was a hardworking hard-ass with a hard body—all of which were true.

Even though Kick had been well vetted, the fact that, to my knowledge, none of us had ever run an op with him still bothered me. I flexed my hand; it was becoming a reflex, and I needed to get it under control. It happened increasingly more often when I was stressed. That couldn't happen while I was undercover.

"Everything okay?" Grinder asked, looking at my right hand.

"Something about this Kick guy isn't sitting right with me."

"What do you want to do?"

"Where's Jagger?"

"Rile asked me to put him and Rage on standby."

"For?"

"If necessary, he wants to send Jagger into Los Aztecas."

I raised a brow. "Interesting call. He plans to send Rage into the Crips?"

"Affirmative."

It made sense to have them available to go undercover in the ABT's biggest allies. "Anything else I should know?"

"Rile thinks it was an inside job. Someone within the ABT wanted Possum taken out."

"Which is why they pinned it on Rebel instead of a rival gang." Possum wasn't important enough for the

ABT to risk a gang war. Instead, they saw the opportunity to pin the murder on someone completely outside that world.

This theory also explained why the ABT didn't try to get to Rebel while she was in jail. They had no reason to want her dead; they wanted to ensure she was the one to take the fall for the murder. The fact that we were working to exonerate her might put her in more danger than she already was. However, that wouldn't stop me from proceeding. It only meant that her level of protection had to be high and airtight.

"Did the two of you discuss my cover?"

"Colonel in the Aryan Nation."

Another thing that made sense. The Aryan brotherhoods were local entities, reporting to the bigger organization—the Nation. They used rank in the same way the military did, with captains, majors, colonels, and generals. The highest rank at any state chapter, like at the ABT, would be a major.

"Someone higher up is pissed about the hit on Possum?"

"That's the idea."

"Did Rile find out if the agency still has someone inside the AN?"

Grinder smiled. "Smoke, and he's been briefed."

I smiled too. Broderick "Smoke" Torcher was the kind of intelligence agent I'd always aspired to be. No offense to my brother or any of the other men on the Invincibles team, but Smoke was a warrior, a renegade, and a bloody genius. Out of anyone I'd ever worked with, or even known of in the field of intelligence, Smoke was born to go undercover in a world as potentially deadly as the Aryan Nation.

"Incoming." Grinder motioned out the front window. "He brought them in dark," he added, laughing as he walked to the garage to open the door.

I shook my head at Rile's chosen mode of transport. Somehow he'd gotten his hands on a flower delivery van.

"Casper, it's good to see you," I said as she came inside, rubbing her arms.

"That damn van was refrigerated in the back. And it's good to see you too, Edge." We exchanged cheek-kisses before I turned to Kick and shook his hand. I wished I could say I felt better after having met him, but it was the opposite. The bad feeling I had, intensified.

A few minutes later, Decker pulled up.

"He doesn't look happy," commented Grinder.

"How can you tell?" It seemed to me that the man always had a scowl on his face.

"He's been happier lately. Since he and Mila got married." Grinder motioned toward the road. "This is unexpected, though."

I turned back to see what Grinder was referring to and was as surprised as he to see the sheriff pull in behind Deck. "Did you know about this?" I asked Rile.

"Yes." He brushed his finger over his lower lip.

I walked over to the table where he was seated and pulled out the chair next to him. "What's he doing here?"

"He received an anonymous tip about the gun."

My eyes met Grinder's. "Where is it?"

"Bloody hell," seethed Rile. "Don't tell me you wankers have done something with it."

"I gave it to Mac to run ballistics."

No one said another word until Decker walked in with Mac.

"Ballistics confirmed that the gun found in Rebel's trunk is the one that killed Possum," said Mac after we'd said hello and made introductions.

"Doesn't prove anything," I muttered, immediately feeling foolish for having done so, particularly when Rile glared at me.

"No, it doesn't," said Mac. "And it hasn't been admitted into evidence yet either."

It was one of the things I liked best about Texas, especially outside of the bigger cities. The sheriff had a hell of a lot more say in how stuff like guns were and weren't logged in.

Rile motioned for us to be seated at the table. "Let's run through this."

"Before we get started, there's something you all should know." All heads turned to Mac.

"Rebel wasn't Possum's first rape, attempted or otherwise. Word from one of my sources is that he was warned about the attention he was drawing to the organization. My guess is that his arrest at the Branch the night he assaulted Rebel was the last straw. He wasn't out of jail twenty-four hours before he was found dead."

"Someone within the ABT arranged for his release," said Grinder.

I looked over at Rile. "Either that or the Aryan Nation. Or both."

He nodded and made a note. "I'll touch base with Smoke."

"Why pin it on Rebel, though? Why not a rival gang?" Casper asked.

"Possum wouldn't be worth a war. All the ABT wanted was to get rid of him." What I also knew and they didn't yet, was what Hammer got out of Rebel that day at the jail. She'd admitted that she wanted to kill Possum. She'd said it had something to do with her mother's death. Maybe somehow the ABT knew that too.

"There's more," said Mac. "Word is there's a splinter group supposedly loyal to Possum."

I scrubbed my face with my hand. If that was the case, our job just got exponentially more difficult. "They'll want revenge for his death." I looked to Rile a second time. "It's imperative we know if we're on track with thinking this was a hit. If we are, we can't go in until we know whether the ABT or AN ordered it."

"Understood."

When Rile left the room, every face at the table looked as solemn as I knew mine did. When he returned a few minutes later, he was brushing his lower lip with his index finger.

"What did you find out?" I asked, too impatient to wait.

"Smoke says the AN didn't call for the hit on Possum."

"Bloody hell," I muttered.

Rile held up his hand again. "Therefore, this mission has two objectives. One, to get the ABT to give up Possum's killer."

"Why would they do that?"

Rather than respond, or even look at me, Rile continued. "The second objective is to neutralize the splinter group." He looked at Casper first and then me. "That's your job and your cover. AN is sending you in because there's chatter about a split in the chapter."

"You think they'll give up Possum's killer in order to smooth things over with AN and then clean their own house?"

Rile's eyes stayed riveted on mine. "Exactly."

If this went the way Rile was suggesting it would, the ABT would not only take care of Possum's killer, but any threat from this splinter group would end too. Whoever they were, they'd all be dead.

17

Rebel

I should've known this whole gig was too good to be true. Or at least too good to last. When Tee-Tee asked me to clear the remaining dishes that a couple of asshat ranch hands had left on the tables in the dining hall, I thought they'd all left.

"I wasn't done with that," I heard a voice say from behind me as I dumped what little food remained on the plate into the garbage.

"Too bad. We're closed until lunch," I said without turning around to look at him.

Within seconds, I felt a tight grip on my arm. "I've been sent with a message, you bitch. Lynch wants you to know that, one way or another, you're gonna pay for what happened to Possum. Call your dogs and your fancy lawyer the fuck off. Ya hear?" He shoved me away from him hard enough that I stumbled into the table behind me and the plates I'd been holding crashed to the floor.

"Que está pasando aqui?" Tee-Tee ran out of the kitchen and over to where I was on my hands and knees picking up broken pieces of glass off the floor. "What happened?"

"That asshole…" I raised my head, but there was no one else in the hall but Tee-Tee and me. I shook my head. "Um, I was cleaning off the tables and ran into someone on his way out. My fault."

"On his way out. Is that what you said?"

I shrugged. "I don't see him now, so he must've been."

"What did he look like?"

"I couldn't tell you."

"I see."

"I'm sorry, Tee-Tee. I'll pay for the broken dishes." She walked away without another word.

She'd told me earlier that once I brought the remaining dirty dishes to the kitchen—the ones that the ranch hands were supposed to bus themselves—I could take a break. We had an hour before we needed to start on prep for the midday meal, which was very little work, considering how few of the cowboys came in for lunch.

As soon as I took the dishes into the kitchen, I took off out the back door, wanting to get as far away from other human beings as I could.

What I really wanted to do was go for a ride, but I'd never ask. Edge had mentioned it briefly at some point. Had that been yesterday? Maybe it was the day before.

I walked through the field, and when I came to a big boulder, I sat down and put my head in my hands. Up until that night at the Long Branch, I would've told you my life was boring. All I'd wanted to do then was get the hell out of Barton Creek and live my life anywhere else. Now, I just wanted to live my life.

I'd give anything to be able to go back to those simple days when I got up and went to work, got off, and went home. I'd hated my life then, but now it was so much worse. How many times had I heard my grandfather tell me to be careful what I wished for? Now I wished I'd listened.

While it wasn't what I'd call hot out, the sun felt warm enough that I closed my eyes and let its rays beat down on my face.

"Well, well, well. Look who's sittin' out here all by her lonesome."

I shielded my eyes and looked up at the same cowboy who'd threatened me earlier. I stood to go back inside, but he grabbed my arm.

"You tell anyone about this, and it isn't just you who's gonna get hurt."

"What does that mean?"

"Figure it out, *Mija*."

18

Edge

I gripped the phone so tightly I expected it might crack. "Where is she now?" I asked Tee-Tee after I answered her call and she told me what had happened in the dining hall.

"Sitting out back. *Pobre niñita.*"

"You think she's lying."

"I do, Edge. I think there was something more to it than her bumping into someone. She said he must have left. Does that sound like *anyone* who works on the ranch?"

It sure as hell didn't. And if someone had seen what went down, whoever the guy was would've been fired and escorted off the property. Not for bumping into Rebel, but for walking away and leaving her to clean up the mess. It wasn't the way the Alexanders did things around here.

"No idea who it was?"

"I didn't see him, but I thought I should call you."

"You did the right thing. I'll be right there." I ended the call. "Where's Decker?" I asked Grinder.

He pointed, looking at me like I was daft.

I stalked over to the same table he'd been seated at earlier. "Rebel had a run-in with a hand in the dining hall. I want to take a look at the security footage to see who it was."

Decker nodded, pulled out his mobile, opened an app, and stood. "Let's go."

I followed him out the front door and into his truck. He peeled out of the driveway and onto the dirt road.

"What's going on, Deck?"

"I need to double-check the footage. He did a good job hiding his face."

"Bloody hell," I muttered.

He had a white-knuckle grip on the steering wheel, and his jaw was as tight as mine felt.

While Decker checked the security equipment at the dining hall, I went in search of Rebel. I needed my eyes on her. Tee-Tee had said she was out back, so that's where I went first. I saw her right away, headed toward me.

"Hey, Rebel."

She shielded her eyes. "Edge. What are you doing here?"

"Let's go inside." Once I made sure the door was closed and locked behind her, I motioned for her to follow me into the dining hall.

"I heard you had a run-in earlier."

"I guess that's what you could call it, since I ran into someone."

"Tee-Tee said that one of the hands bumped into you and then left."

"That's right."

"What did he look like?"

"I didn't get a good look at him. What's with the questions, Edge? I broke a couple of plates."

"I think there was more to it."

Her eyes stayed steady on mine. "There wasn't."

She was lying to me, and I didn't like it. "I need to find Decker. When I get back, there are some things I want to talk over with you."

"Like what?"

"For starters, I want to make sure you're armed. Do you know how to handle a gun, Rebel?"

She stared at me and cocked her head.

"If you don't, I'll teach you."

"Sometimes it's very obvious you're not from Texas, Edge. Do I know how to handle a gun?"

I put my hand around her arm, and she flinched. "What was that?"

"What do you mean?"

"You flinched."

"No, I didn't."

Now I was livid. Her lies were piling up. "What did he do to you? Show me."

"Edge—"

I took her hand instead of touching her arm again. "Come on. Let's go."

"You said you had to find Decker."

"It can wait." I realized that I'd ridden here with Decker, and the truck was back at the house. "On second thought, stay right here."

"I have work to do, Edge. We have to get ready for lunch."

"Not today, you won't be."

She put her hands on her hips. "What did you say?"

I stalked back over and got in her face. "I said, you won't be working today."

"Who the fuck do you think you are?"

"I'm the fucking man you're lying to, and we're getting to the bottom of why."

"You're making way too much of a couple of plates."

"Am I? Are you absolutely certain of that, Rebel? Tell me this. If you or someone else gets hurt because you aren't willing to tell me what really happened, will I still be making too much of it?"

She didn't answer. Didn't so much as move her head.

"Wait here. Do…not…move."

I flexed my hand as I walked away. The damn thing had been spasming the whole time I talked to Rebel, only serving to make me angrier. If she was in danger, if someone on the ranch had the ability to get to her, my bloody hand *had* to work. I had to be able to fire my fucking gun.

I couldn't find Decker, so I rang him. "Where are you?"

"Office."

"Have you figured out who it was?"

"Yep. I'm scanning the rest of the feeds for him now. My fear is he's already left the property."

"And if he hasn't?"

"I'm putting the entire ranch on high alert. Full throttle protocol."

"I'm taking Rebel back to the house. I need your truck."

"Go ahead. I'll let you know when I find the *sonuvabitch*."

When I got back to the kitchen, Rebel wasn't where I'd told her to wait. I pulled out my mobile and opened the tracking app. She was almost back to the house, and that meant there would be hell to pay.

19

Rebel

As I walked into the bedroom, I felt a tear slide down my cheek and cursed my damn self-pity. I threw myself on the bed and pounded my fists into the pillow, hating how powerless I felt.

The whole way back to the house, I went back and forth. Edge knew I was lying to him, but the guy who was sent to threaten me had made it perfectly clear that Tee-Tee would be the one in danger if I divulged what he'd said.

So what the fuck was I supposed to do? I rolled to my back and stared up at the ceiling. What had the guy said that was any different from what I already knew? I'd been arrested for murdering Possum. Wasn't that me paying? And if I somehow got exonerated, wouldn't that mean Edge or someone else had found the real killer? In which case, wouldn't that person pay? How the fuck was I supposed to call "my dogs" and lawyer off if I couldn't tell anyone what he'd said?

I wished instead of trying to walk away, I'd kicked the fucker in the balls. Done *something*. At least then I'd feel more like myself.

I hit my forehead with the palm of my hand. This wasn't who I was. I was never the girl who sat around and let bad things happen either to myself or anyone I cared about. I was Lucy-fucking-Rebel-Marks. I climbed out of bed, went into the closet, and looked for my clothes. Not the little Mary Sunshine shit that woman had given me. My shit.

I laughed as I stripped, thinking about Edge asking me if I knew how to handle a gun. Someday, when I managed to get out from under all the crap that had descended on my life, I'd show him exactly how much better I handled a gun than he did. Okay, well, maybe that was stretching it. Edge was a goddamn spy. He better be able to handle a weapon better than me.

I was about to pull my boots on when I heard Edge walk into the bedroom.

"Rebel?" he called out.

"What?"

He turned on the light I hadn't bothered with. "What in the bloody hell do you think you're doing?"

I brushed past him. "I'm going back to work."

"No. You're not."

I spun around on him. "Yeah. I am."

"I told you before, you aren't working for the rest of the day. Even if you showed up, Tee-Tee would send you back here."

"You have no right."

"I have *every* right. You're in my custody. It's my job to keep you safe."

I took a step forward and got in his face. "Just because you posted my bail, doesn't mean you own me. And if that's what you think, then take me back to jail right this minute. I've been on my own a long goddamn time, and I don't—"

Fuck! He did it again. The bastard grabbed my neck and kissed me. Just like every other time, it was hard and deep and long. Also like the other times, my goddamn traitorous body melted against his like I didn't have a brain in my head…or any pride. Somehow, I willed my arms to work and pushed against him. "Don't do that!" I shouted.

He got right back in my face. "You're so fucking hot when you're angry. I can't keep my bloody hands off you as it is, but when you—"

This time I grabbed his neck and plastered my mouth against his. Fuck if he didn't light a fire in me, especially when he got all demanding and threatened me with consequences. I kissed the shit out of him, and he gave it right back to me.

As if every part of my body suddenly operated independently of my brain, I began ripping at his clothes. I wanted Edge naked, and I wanted it right now.

I tore at his shirt, and once he took over and threw it to the ground, I clawed at his belt buckle. Why in the hell were these things so damn hard to unfasten? Weren't guys ever in a hurry when they had to take a piss?

I took a step back and watched as Edge shed the rest of the clothes he was wearing and then stalked toward me.

"You better fucking want this, Rebel, because it's going to be bloody hard for me to stop if you don't."

"You stop and I swear to God…"

He ran his hand through his hair and took a deep breath.

"I'm warning you, Edge. Don't you dare hold back on me. I want everything you've got. You promised you'd take care of me. You said you'd wring me out and then come back for more. Don't even think about disappointing me."

Edge closed the short distance between us like a bull. Between the two of us, I was naked moments later. He picked me up, threw my ass on the bed, and crawled on top of me.

"Put your hands above your head," he growled, wedging his knee between my legs and then spreading them wider with his hands.

He shifted his body down and blew his warm breath on my already-overheated pussy. When I moved my hand to grab his head, it was like lightning the way he grasped it. "Over your head, Rebel, and don't move. If you can't do as I ask, I'll force you."

A flood of arousal gushed from me. "How?" He hesitated and I wanted to cry. I thrashed instead. *"How, goddammit?"*

When he shook his head, I tried to get out from under him, but he was too strong. "I'm going to bind you, Rebel."

I stared into his eyes. "Do it."

He straddled me like he had before. "Do. Not. Move." He climbed off me and was back in less than a minute. "Close your eyes and keep them closed."

He took my wrist in his hand, wrapped something soft around it, and then pulled it taut. As much as I wanted to see where he'd tied it off, there was no way I'd open my eyes and give him a reason to stop. He did the same with my other wrist.

I waited in anticipation for what he'd do next, never dreaming that I'd feel his hand wrap something around my ankle.

"Do not open your eyes," he warned, as if he'd read my mind and knew I was about to. I squeezed my lids shut. My breathing accelerated when I felt him bind my other ankle.

His hands grasped my waist as his mouth landed on my drenched pussy. He dragged his tongue through my slit again and again. When he stopped, I squeezed my eyes again in a desperate attempt not to look to see what he'd do next.

"Open them," he demanded instead, and I did. He rested his cheek against my belly and smiled. "You're all mine now, little Rebel, and I intend to wring every ounce of pleasure there is out of this hot…fucking… body."

"Please," I begged, trying to stop from writhing beneath him.

He raised his head. "Where shall I begin?"

"Where you were works for me."

He smiled and shook his head. "You forgot your consequences. You don't get to choose, Rebel."

Over the course of what felt like hours, Edge painstakingly slowly got to know every inch of my body. He used his lips, his tongue, his hands, his fingers. Every time I was close to coming, he stopped what he was doing, waited a few seconds, and then began his assault somewhere else.

My nipples ached. My pussy throbbed. I was almost crying I wanted to come so badly. When I felt as though I was about to lose my mind, Edge made it worse by moving away from me.

"No," I cried.

"No?" he asked, holding up a condom. "Are you certain?"

"No. I mean, yes. Please. God. Edge. Please."

He smiled. "If you're sure."

"Please," I moaned again.

"Are you ready for me?" he asked, thrusting long, thick fingers inside me. "Yes. I believe you are."

I wanted to close my eyes again and focus only on how it felt when Edge was finally inside me, but I couldn't. I was mesmerized by his every movement. He was as graceful as he was powerful. At the same moment I felt his hardness at my opening, he leaned forward and bit my nipple. I cried out in pain at the exact moment he thrust into me, and the orgasm that he'd held at bay came crashing through me.

He fucked me harder, longer, deeper than anyone ever had before, each thrust more powerful than the last.

I longed to touch him, wrap my arms around him, feel the muscles in his ass flex as his cock pounded into me. Before I could ask him to release my hands, it was as though something in him let loose. What I'd thought was his all before, felt soft compared to the way he fucked me now. When he bit my other nipple and I cried out like I had earlier, he roared. "You are mine, Rebel. Mine. Do you understand?"

"Take me, Edge. Take all of me," I cried as he thrust harder and harder into me. "I want to touch you. Let me touch you," I pleaded.

He slowed with my words, and I wanted to cry for him to keep moving.

"You will, little Rebel. I told you, tonight I'll wring every ounce of pleasure from this body. And when I'm done, we'll begin again. Whatever you want, you'll have." He stopped moving completely and stared into my eyes. "And whatever I want, I'll have too."

He thrust into me again, slowly at first and then picking up the rhythm until he was slamming into me. "Come with me," he growled and I did, clenching him with my body as I felt him shudder and pulse inside me.

My sweaty body chilled when he rolled away, and I groaned.

"I'll just be a second." True to his word, he was right back, untying both my legs, rubbing each one in turn before releasing my arms and doing the same to them.

Once he had, he lay on his back. "Come here." He pulled me on top of him. My legs on his; my stomach on his; my breasts against his chest; my head resting on his shoulder.

He wrapped his arms around me and squeezed. "You feel so fucking good."

"So do you," I murmured.

With one hand, he brushed my hair from my face. "Kiss me, Rebel."

I did. Starting with where my mouth rested against his pulse, working my way down the length of his body and then back up again. Finally, my lips met his. Edge grabbed the back of my neck and thrust his tongue in my mouth, kissing me longer, deeper, and harder than he ever had before.

"Fucking amazing," he whispered, stroking the side of my face with his finger. "You felt it too, right?"

Felt it? My body hummed with it. Every muscle screamed in exhaustion, and yet I wanted more. I doubted I'd ever get enough of Edge, and with that thought, my eyes filled with tears.

20

Edge

I hated that Rebel was crying, but I felt that if I asked her about it, I'd only make it worse. After sex like we'd just experienced, part of me wanted to cry too. It was that good. That mind-blowing. That earth-shattering. That gut-wrenchingly brilliant.

The sun was setting, which meant dinner was over. I'd get no argument about going back to the dining hall. I studied the bruises on her arm where someone had obviously grabbed her. I still wanted answers, and I'd bloody well get them, but not now. First, I had to get her to tell me why she was crying.

I tried to wait to let her be the first to speak, but the longer she remained silent, the less I could stop myself from giving her comfort. I put my fingertips on her chin and lifted her face so I could see her eyes, even if they were closed. I touched her cheek with the pad of my thumb, wishing I could climb inside her brain, dance around in her head, and know everything that made this little rebel tick.

She was so fierce, so on fire earlier, that I was powerless not to kiss her. Fucking her? Jesus, it was every dream I'd had of her come true. Her body, while slight, felt so goddamn perfect under me. The memory of the look on her exquisite face every time she went crashing into ecstasy made me steel-hard again and again—including now.

But there was so much more. I wanted to know everything about the woman I held in my arms. What little I did know barely scratched the surface, and yet, there was a part of me that felt as though I'd known her forever.

She was passionately independent, but what choice did she have? She was alone in the world. *Was.* Not any longer. From now on, she had me. I knew in my heart it wouldn't be easy to convince her she did. She'd fight it. Fight me every step of the way. She'd tell herself she wasn't good enough for me, when in reality, I didn't hold a candle to this mesmerizing creature.

"I want to be a part of your life, Rebel," I blurted.

Her body shuddered. I flipped us both over and rested my elbows above her shoulders. Her eyes were closed, but I could see her. As I told her what I wanted, I'd be able to watch her expression, gauge her fear.

"I'm not going to fall by the wayside."

She shook her head from side to side; she didn't believe me.

"Look into my eyes." It took a while, but finally, she did. "I want to be in your life. Not just today. Not just until we exonerate you. Not just until you think I've had my fill of you and you decide it'll be easier if you leave me first. I'll still be in your life, sweetness. I'm staying, and I want you to stay too."

She looked away.

"Tell me you believe me," I demanded, knowing damn well she didn't. She wouldn't lie either. Not now. Not about this. If I could get her to speak, she'd tell me I was crazy. She might even say it wasn't what she wanted. I longed for her to hand me every argument, just so I could dispute each one.

What she said, though, was the last thing I expected.

Her eyes bored into mine. "I don't need you, Edge. I know you think I do, but I don't. Earlier, when you came into the bedroom and I told you I was going to work…a few minutes before that, I woke up. Since the day I was arrested, I'd let myself escape into a trance. It allowed me to keep breathing, keep putting one foot in front of the other, without looking too far into the future."

She laughed. "I even fantasized that you'd show up and get me out of jail. My fantasy did not involve you posting bail, though; it was more that you broke me out."

I laughed too, loving the lines etched into her face when she smiled.

"My point is, you don't have to save me, Edge. I'm capable of saving myself."

Was that what I really wanted deep down? Was it just about saving her? I didn't think it was, but it was significant enough of a thought to consider.

"I need you to not do this for me."

"What do you mean?"

"I need to be an active participant in every facet of my life. It's the only way I can make it through this and keep the most important parts of myself intact."

"Explain so I understand better."

"I need to be the one who figures out who really killed Possum."

I didn't respond right away, because I didn't know how. I couldn't imagine a way to make that happen. Even I didn't plan to find the killer myself. I didn't expect it would take long either. In fact, if he'd been able to make contact with Smoke, Rile might already have a name.

"I want you to tell me what's going on, Edge. Everything. I don't want you to hold back a single detail."

I rolled from her body and sat up, resting against the bed's headboard. She sat up too and folded her legs, giving me a direct view of her glistening pussy.

"Sweetness," I murmured, unable to tear my eyes away.

"Oh." She unfolded her legs, pressed them together, and stretched them out in front of her. I wished I hadn't spoken, but even if I hadn't, she would've noticed I wasn't looking where I should be. Even now, I couldn't. Her pebbled nipples were calling out for my mouth to feast on them.

"Edge!"

I averted my eyes, but like beacons, her perfect tits recaptured my gaze.

"It isn't any easier for me, you know."

When I looked up, she was looking directly at my quickly hardening cock. "Maybe we should put some clothes on." I reached for my boxer briefs and pulled them on. When I grabbed my shirt, she took it out of my hands and put it over her head.

Her cheeks pinkened. "I like looking at the rest of you."

"Are you sure you can resist?" I couldn't help but flex my muscles.

"I'll let you know if it becomes too much for me."

She crossed her legs again.

"You must wear knickers, sweetness. Otherwise, there is no way in the world I can look anywhere else."

She smirked, rose from the bed, and was back a minute later. When she sat cross-legged again, I could see the ones she chose were pink. I wasn't sure I'd fare much better with knickers. The idea of ripping them from her body with my teeth had my cock equally as hard as seeing her pussy had done. I grabbed the throw and tossed it over her lap. "I'm sorry, sweetness, but I can't concentrate if your legs are open like that."

She smirked again, which I adored. It was dawning on me that there was a lot I adored about this woman.

Suddenly, it was like a switch inside her had turned off. Instead of playful and flirty, she looked as though she was preparing for a kill.

"There are things I need to tell you, Edge."

"I need you to tell me the truth, Rebel. All of it."

"I will. I promise."

"Go ahead."

"Do you remember when Hammer asked if I wanted to kill Possum?"

I did. In fact, it was something that lingered in the back of my mind. "Yes," I answered.

"He asked me what my motive was, and I told him that Possum killed my mother."

I nodded, almost afraid to speak. In fact, I found myself struggling to get enough air in my lungs.

"I also told you my mother was a meth addict."

Again, I nodded.

"For the first five years of my life, my mother and I both lived with my grandparents. I don't remember much from that time. We were on our own for a while, she and my grandparents were on the outs. I don't know why, but I can guess. Anyway, when I was eleven, I took off and went back to my grandparents' house." Rebel took a deep breath. "She didn't come after me. Part of me thought she would, I guess. In the end, it was for the best, even though that was hard for me to understand at the time."

I tried to picture an eleven-year-old Rebel. I'd be willing to bet she was the quintessential tomboy.

"Between the time we originally moved out of my grandparents' house until the time I took off and went back, my mom left me alone a lot. I learned to fend for myself. It was up to me to get myself up and to school, up to me to try to find something to eat.

"That's when I met Blanca. She and I became best friends, and she began to notice that I never had anything to eat at lunch. She must've told Tee-Tee, because soon after that, Blanca started bringing two sandwiches instead of one, two bags of chips. Anyway, I'm getting sidetracked."

I reached over and held her hand. She took it as if it were a lifeline.

"Fast forward to me graduating from high school. My mom showed up, surprisingly. By then it was just me and my granddaddy. My grandma died not long after I moved in with them. Cancer."

She blinked at tears that threatened to spill over her cheeks. The pain of losing her grandmother obviously sat very close to the surface of her emotions.

"My mom looked good. Better than I remembered her ever looking. Later, I learned that my grandfather had managed to get her into rehab."

Rebel took a deep breath. "This is a lot harder than I thought it would be."

"You don't have to do this, sweetness. I'm willing to listen, and I want to know more about your life, but I don't want you to feel forced to tell me things you're not ready to talk about."

"I need to do this, Edge. It's already eating away at me. If I don't tell you the whole story, I think it might consume me."

21

Rebel

I got up from the bed and grabbed the photo of my mom and me that had been taken right after my high school graduation.

"We had four, almost five, great years. Mom was clean, and I got to know her. Blanca died when we were both seventeen. It was the same age my mother was when she started using. I always found that signif-icant somehow. My mom had long stretches where she was clean, like when she was pregnant with me."

I looked into Edge's eyes, wondering what he must be thinking about me. He was from England; I was the illegitimate daughter of a meth-head. And I hadn't even gotten to the bad part of the story yet. Should I even continue?

I already knew the answer to my own question. I had to. Even if he wanted nothing to do with me after I told him, what I'd said about it eating me alive, I meant. I couldn't hold it in any longer.

"The night you pulled Possum off me…it was no accident that I was with him."

That didn't come out right, but it was accurate enough.

Edge looked into my eyes and squeezed my hand. "Tell me the rest of the story, Rebel."

"I was waitressing at the Barton Creek Diner. So was my mom. She'd actually gotten me the job. We were living together in the apartment where I lived before I was arrested."

His gaze stayed steady on mine; it was unnerving.

"I came home from work one night. It was late, almost midnight. Mom had the night off. I parked in the same place I always did, where we found Susan the day you got me out of jail."

He nodded but didn't press me even once to hurry it up.

"As I walked up to the building, there was a man coming out. There was something about him, like I could feel the evil coming off him in waves. There wasn't much light, but as we passed each other, our eyes met. I'll never forget his. They were almost all black, hardly any white around his pupils at all. I remember feeling sick to my stomach. I just knew something was wrong. I raced up the stairs and into our apartment."

I let go of Edge's hand and wrapped my arms around my waist, feeling just as sick as I did that night.

"Do you need to take a break?"

I shook my head. "Let me get this part out."

"Go ahead."

"I burst into the apartment and didn't see my mom anywhere and then noticed the bathroom door was closed. I called out to her, and as soon as she answered, I knew she was high. The door was locked, and I pounded on it, yelling for her to open it."

I covered my face with my hands. I couldn't tell him the rest. I'd said it out loud only once in my life, and that had been too much for me.

"Did your mum overdose, Rebel?" he asked, perhaps sensing I couldn't go on.

"Yes." There was more to the story, what had happened between the time I pounded on the bathroom door and less than an hour later when I found her. Most of it, I didn't remember. "He gave her the drugs."

Edge nodded again. "That is a logical assumption."

I shook my head as a torrent of tears spilled onto my cheeks. "He admitted it. That night, in the parking lot. He laughed about it."

Edge lay back on the bed, against the pillows, and pulled me into his arms. I rested my head against his beating heart, wishing I knew what he was thinking but, at the same time, dreading it.

"Let me see if I can piece the rest of this together."

I couldn't have spoken even if I wanted to. I was crying too hard.

"Possum showed up at the Long Branch. Did he recognize you?"

I shook my head.

"Your intention was to kill him, but it didn't go as planned."

I was stunned at how one simple sentence conveyed exactly what happened that night.

"I lured him out there. I had a gun, but I wasn't strong enough to fight him once he realized what was about to happen. He knocked the gun away and tried to rape me instead."

Edge's eyes bored into mine. I so wanted to know what he was thinking. What he said next was not at all what I thought he would.

"Earlier, you said you wanted to know what was happening with finding Possum's killer."

"I do."

He ran his fingers through my hair. "Some of what I have to tell you, might be difficult to hear."

"I have to know, Edge."

22

Edge

I scrubbed my face with my hand. This was a first for me. I would never have been tempted to talk about a job outside of the team, but as she'd said, this was her life. I was still reeling from her admission that she'd intended to kill Possum. I couldn't let myself think about how close she'd come to death that night. Instead of just killing her, Possum had decided to rape her first. When I came along, I'd actually saved her life.

I took a deep breath. "As you know, Possum was connected to the Aryan Brotherhood of Texas."

Rebel nodded.

"What you might not know is he had prior rape arrests. Evidently, he was in trouble with the Aryan Nation, the parent organization, because of it."

I watched as Rebel processed what I was telling her.

"We believe that his arrest the night of your attempted rape, triggered a hit. You, Steel, and I played into the setup. I'd even go so far as to say that someone made sure Possum not only got out of jail two days later, but showed up at the Branch the night he did."

"They set it up so I'd be the one to take the fall for his murder?"

"That's right."

"If you find Possum's real killer, what does that mean for me?"

"First, it means you're exonerated. The second part is more difficult."

"Second part?"

"According to the sheriff, Possum had a following, and they're not happy about his death. Since they believe the hit came down either from the leadership of the ABT or from the Nation, there's talk of them breaking off."

Rebel turned her head so I could see her face. She was ghostly pale. "They blame me."

I nodded. "It was inevitable, in my opinion. Possum was a serial rapist."

"But it was me that got him arrested."

"I'm afraid so."

"Fuck." Rebel sat up first and then stood. "Finding Possum's killer isn't my biggest problem, is it?"

"Given we have someone on the inside of the Aryan Nation, we may soon have that answer. What our team is referring to as the second objective, may not be."

"What is it?"

"Neither ABT nor AN is going to be happy when they learn of this break-off group. Our hope is to identify them and let their own organization handle it from there."

"Kill them?"

"I don't know exactly."

She sat back down on the bed. "You said your hope is to identify who the break-off group is."

"That's right."

"How? I mean, how would you go about doing that?"

"A team will go undercover."

"Into the ABT?"

"That's right." Why was she asking? Something told me I wasn't going to want to know.

"Who are they?"

A question I never would've considered answering if asked by any other "civilian."

"Two of our best. Me and Casper."

"You?"

I nodded.

"Why can't this Casper go in alone?"

"We'll go in as a couple." When she raised her brows, I added, "Casper is a woman."

"I want to do it."

"Do what?"

"I want to be the person who goes in with you."

There were two reasons that wouldn't work. First, she had absolutely no training. More importantly, the ABT knew who she was.

"They'll know who you are the minute you walk in the door."

"Right." She slowly closed her eyes and then reopened them. "I want to meet her."

Her statement confused me. "Casper?"

Rebel nodded.

"Now or after it's over?"

"Now."

"Not possible."

"Then, I'll do it my way." Rebel stood and walked out of the room, leaving me in stunned silence. What in the bloody hell did that mean?

23

Rebel

I expected Edge to join me in the kitchen where I was pacing, but after several minutes, he still hadn't come out of the bedroom. Finally, when he did, it looked as though he was ending a call.

His eyes pierced mine as he stalked toward me. "I don't understand why you want to meet Casper, but I'm willing to make a deal with you."

"What?"

"You want to meet her? You can under one condition."

"Like I said, what?"

"You tell me the truth about what went on today. Not just me, the rest of the team too."

"Okay."

"The truth, Rebel. All of it."

"I just said okay."

Edge walked outside and sat in a chair on the patio. I was unsure whether I should follow. Eventually, I did. "Are you angry?"

"Oh, yeah. Bloody mad as hell."

"Then, why do it?"

"I told you before. I want to be a part of your life."

"You could've said no."

He shook his head. "I couldn't. This is me showing you that when I say I want to be part of your life, I mean it."

"You hardly know me."

For the first time since I came outside, he looked at me. "Is that really the way you feel? That we hardly know each other?"

I shrugged. "It hasn't even been a week, Edge."

"That's irrelevant." When I rolled my eyes, he glared at me. "Don't do that."

"Roll my eyes?"

"Make light of what I'm saying to you just because you're insecure." He looked back out into the darkness, and I turned to leave. Before I crossed over the threshold, Edge spoke again.

"Go ahead, Rebel. Go inside. Be angry with me. When you're over it, I'll still be here."

"You don't know me as well as you think."

"Don't I?" He stood and walked inside; I followed.

"If you knew me like you think you do, you'd understand why I have to do this."

He shook his head. "And if you stopped thinking only of yourself for a moment, you'd see that it's because I do know you that I agreed to something I am fundamentally opposed to."

When he walked into the room with all the computer monitors and closed the door, I went into the bedroom and grabbed my denim jacket. There was something about wearing my own damn clothes that made me feel like…myself.

Fuck him for saying I was insecure. He had no clue what my life had been like. My mother chose meth over me, and my grandmother died less than a year after I moved in with her and my grandfather, who did the best he could, but he didn't know dick about raising a girl like me. He sure as hell didn't know anything about discipline. The worst thing he ever said to me was that he was disappointed in me. In a way, that worked.

Edge and I were different. While I didn't know much, other than that he was from England, the way he spoke and carried himself made it evident he was in a different class. I guessed his parents were rich. It was probably the reason he didn't care about money. The only time someone cared about money was when they didn't have it. I'd *admitted* he was out of my league. Just because I was smart enough to realize it, didn't mean I was insecure. Did it?

God, why did his opinion have to matter so goddamn much? I'd always been okay with who I was, where I came from, and what I wanted out of life. Hadn't I?

Or did the fact that all I'd wanted was to get out of Barton Creek, any way I could, mean that he was right?

I walked back outside and sat in the chair Edge had been sitting in earlier and thought about the other things he'd said. He could've flat-out refused to let me talk to anyone, but he didn't. What he'd been trying to tell me was that he had enough respect for me to do what I'd asked even though he was against it. I'd been too busy thinking only of myself to realize it.

When I went to find him to apologize, I saw him just inside the back door with a woman who had to be Casper. Neither heard me, so I stood and watched as they embraced. Instead of pulling away, he rested his forehead against hers like he'd done with me a couple of times. They were talking too quietly for me to hear what about, and neither was making a move to break away from the other. I couldn't move without them noticing or hearing me, so instead of trying to sneak off, like I wanted to do more than anything, I cleared my throat.

Casper was the first to break the embrace. Edge motioned for me to come closer.

"Rebel, meet Casper."

"Nice to meet you."

She didn't shake my outstretched hand. In fact, she looked at me with complete disinterest.

"Where's everyone else?" I asked Edge.

"A few minutes out. Why don't we wait in here?" He motioned toward the computer room, and with his hand on the small of Casper's back, he led her inside, expecting me to follow, I guess. Part of me wanted to walk the other way.

She leaned against the desk and tucked her hair back on one side, revealing that beneath the long, dark, almost-black locks, the side of her head was shaved.

She had on a leather jacket but shrugged it off. Underneath, she wore what looked more like a camisole than a top. I inwardly smiled, thinking it was exactly the kind of thing I'd wear. One of her buff arms was covered in lightly colored but elaborate tattoos. Her other arm was bare. She wasn't as tall as me, but I wouldn't call her short either. She was compact. Every visible muscle was toned, giving me no reason to think what was beneath her clothes was any different.

Edge's cell rang and he excused himself. "Be nice," he muttered as he walked past me and closed the door behind him.

Without that comment, I might have been. Now? No way in hell. "Did you fuck him?"

The disinterested look on Casper's face left, and she looked me in the eye, maybe for the first time. "I don't like swearing."

Wait. What did she just say? "Excuse me?"

"Stop with the swearing, or I'll walk out of here."

"Answer my question."

"That isn't any of your fucking business."

"I thought you didn't like swearing."

"I don't like it when other people do it."

We stood in silence until I couldn't stand it any longer. "I'm not the kind of person who can sit back and do nothing while my fate is in someone else's hands."

"Then get out of the fucking way and let us do our jobs."

"To you, it's a job. To me, it's my life."

She raised her chin and glared at me.

"I didn't kill Possum—"

"I'm aware." She looked down at her perfectly manicured fingernails.

"*And* my understanding is that whether I killed him or not, doesn't matter. The fact that I got him arrested for attempted rape is what set everything in motion."

She continued glaring at me but didn't speak.

"Someone threatened me today. Or delivered a threat. They told me that one way or another I'd pay for Possum's death. I can't live the rest of my life looking over my shoulder. I have to find out who these people are."

I could hear voices on the other side of the door; the rest of the team must've arrived.

She stood and put her hand on the knob.

"Wait."

She didn't turn around, but she didn't walk out either.

"I'm not very good at letting people help me. Not that that's what you're doing, but I'm used to no one taking care of me but me."

"You have the best guy there is in the world looking out for you. Accept it. Appreciate it. Don't fuck it up."

"What happened between the two of you?"

"Ask him."

Instead of us walking out, Edge came back in with Decker and two other men. "Rebel, this is Grinder and Rile."

"We're on limited time," said Decker. "Tell us what happened today."

I told them about the man bumping into me in the dining hall and saying I'd pay for Possum's death, and that he found me outside later and threatened that if I told anyone what he'd said, I wouldn't be the only one who got hurt. "He made it clear he meant Tee-Tee."

"Anything else?" Edge asked.

I nodded. "He said a name. *Lynch* wanted me to know that I'd pay one way or another."

I watched as Edge looked between the three men and one other woman in the room. "Anything else you want to ask?"

After no one spoke up, they all walked out.

I stayed where I was, eyes closed, arms folded. I could hear Edge in the kitchen after the others left. Part of me wished he would've left with them.

I couldn't get the image out of my head of him and Casper embracing when they didn't know I was looking. If I went out and faced him now, I knew that instead of keeping my mouth shut like I should, I'd do the same thing to him that I did to Casper and ask if he'd fucked her.

But did I really need to ask? The embrace I saw sure made it appear that way. Maybe he had women on circulation. One in. One out. I happened to be in now, but soon I'd be out, just like Casper.

I hated feeling jealous as much as I hated self-pity.

I rolled my shoulders and stood. Just because I had to leave this room, didn't mean I had to talk to Edge. I walked out, stormed past him, and stalked down the hall and into his bedroom. Once there, I went into the closet and grabbed the clothes Shadow had given me. I took them into the guest room, threw them on the bed, and went back for more. This time, I grabbed the photos I'd put on his bookshelves. Next, I'd get the boxes that contained the rest of my possessions.

When I got to the bedroom door, Edge stood in the threshold, barring my exit. "What are you doing?"

"I don't like staying in here. It creeps me out."

He raised his brow. "Creeps you out? Never heard that one before."

"Please get out of my way."

When he reached for me, I wrenched away and, in the process, dropped my framed photos. The glass of two of the four shattered on the wood floor.

My stupid eyes filled with tears when I bent down to pick them up, and he pushed my hands away.

"Let me do this. I don't want you to cut yourself."

"They're *mine*."

He sat back on his haunches. "I know they are. I'm just trying to help you."

"But…" *Fuck. Goddammit.* If I said another word, I wouldn't be able to stop from crying.

Edge grasped my wrists and pulled me up and away from the broken glass. Once I was on my feet, he picked me up and carried me out to the family room.

He set me on the sofa and then sat next to me. "What's going on, Rebel?"

I looked up at the ceiling, trying to keep my tears from sliding down my cheeks. When I failed, he reached out and brushed them away.

"Tell me why you're upset."

"Why didn't you tell me Casper was your girlfriend?"

His eyebrows rose. "What's this, then?"

"I saw you embracing her."

This time he nodded. "I see. So you assumed she was my…*girlfriend*?"

"Lover? Does that define your relationship more accurately?"

"Is that why you wanted to meet her? You're jealous?"

"Wrong. I'm annoyed. You lied to me."

"When did I lie?"

I repeated his words verbatim. *"What you said earlier, 'Rebel, about my treating other women the way I'm treating you tonight, I haven't. Not ever.'"*

"Do you want to know the true nature of my relationship with Casper?"

I tried to get up, but he pinned me to the sofa by putting an arm on each side of me. "Hell, no."

"You'd rather continue believing falsehoods so you have a reason to stay angry with me?"

"I'm not interested in a play-by-play. Thanks, but no thanks."

"I want you to wait here while I clean up the glass."

"I can do it myself."

He took a deep breath. "Rebel, I said to wait here."

I was furious with him, but when he used that tone of voice, I couldn't help but fall into line. I hated it as much as I loved it.

When he came back, he was carrying my photos along with a couple of other frames I didn't recognize.

"What are you doing?" I asked when I saw him removing his own photos and replacing them with mine.

"I'll get new ones another day."

"You don't have to do that."

"I want you to be able to look at the photos of the people whose memory brings you peace."

My eyes filled with tears again. "Why do you have to be so sweet?"

He looked up at me, smiled, and handed me one of the photos he'd removed. "There was a time in my life when looking at these was the only way I could find my own peace."

I pointed to the young boy. "This looks like you."

"'Tis me." He pointed to the older boy. "That's my brother, Lennox. And those two people are my mum and dad."

Each of them looked perfect. And happy. Perfectly happy. "You have a lovely family."

"I did, at one time. No longer."

"What do you mean?"

Edge pushed up the sleeve of his shirt and turned his arm over. He pointed to the tattoo I'd noticed the first night I met him. "Annaliese and Arlo are my parents, and this"—he pointed to the date—"is the day we lost them."

I gasped and covered my mouth with my hand. "I'm so sorry. I thought…"

He looked into my eyes. "I almost died then too. Poor Lennox. He lost his parents and immediately became one."

I reached out and cupped his cheek with my palm. "I don't know what to say."

He covered my hand with his. "I was in hospital for several weeks. Lennox gave up going to university to become my guardian. Not just that. He rarely left my side."

"You were all he had."

"And vice versa." He rubbed his finger over the image. "He was here a few days ago but is in Boston now, hopefully a soon-to-be happily married man."

I smiled. "Yeah?"

"Yes." He smiled too, but it left quickly. "It's one year today since Casper lost her husband."

I closed my eyes.

"I knew it would be a difficult day for her. I even suggested we shouldn't send her in. She wanted it. Told me that as long as she was working, she'd keep her mind off what happened."

"And because of me—"

Edge put his fingertips on my lips. "Don't. Nothing about this is your fault, Rebel."

"What happened to him?"

"He was an agent too. An op went south, and he got caught in the crossfire."

"Like you did." I put my hand on his arm.

"I was a luckier bloke."

"I wish I could tell her how sorry I am."

"You'll have a chance when this is all over." He rolled his shoulders, and I knew he had more to say; I dreaded whatever it was. "I'd like to propose something to you."

Here it came. "What?"

"If there's something you're feeling uncertain about, just ask me. I told you I'd never lie to you, Rebel, and I meant it."

"I'm sorry I was such a bitch…to both of you."

"I know how you can make it up to me."

"Yeah? Does it involve me on—"

"Make me one of those cakes."

24

Edge

"Tomorrow," I added, picking Rebel up and carrying her into my bedroom. There was no way in hell I'd let her sleep anywhere but with me.

"Why do you always carry me? I can walk."

"I told you I like feeling you in my arms."

She sighed and rested her head on my shoulder. If someone had told me earlier that's what she'd do, I would've called them a bloody liar.

"My clothes are in the other room."

"You won't be needing clothes."

"I won't?" she asked in a voice unlike any I'd heard from her to this point. "Why won't I?"

I laughed at her playfulness, but the truth was, it warmed my heart. "This way, little Rebel." I motioned with my head toward the bath.

I recognized the chime of her mobile before she did.

"What's that?"

"A text from Tee-Tee," I answered, picking it up and handing it to her.

"How do you know it's from her?"

"I programmed it."

"Yeah? Did you program a particular chime for you?"

"Maybe."

"What is it?"

"You'll have to wait until I ring you to find out."

Rebel smiled and then read Tee-Tee's text. "It says she expects me to be back at work tomorrow morning." She typed something on the screen with her finger.

"What was your response?"

"That I'd see her early, but not bright."

I cocked my head.

"You know, before dawn."

Every so often, Rebel gave me the gift of seeing her the way she was when she was younger. It wasn't often that she was playful or silly.

Whether it had anything to do with me or not, I took part of the credit. If she didn't feel comfortable around me, truly didn't trust me, she'd never let me see that side of her.

When I woke sometime in the middle of the night, Rebel wasn't in bed next to me; she was sitting by the window. It was still dark, but she'd lit a single candle.

Her shadow fell on the wall, an outline of her perfect shape. I watched her body rise and fall with a heavy sigh as she fingered the brocade fabric of the cushion on which she sat.

I watched as her eyes closed and she raised her chin. It looked almost as though she was speaking, but silently. Again, I wished I could crawl inside her brain, know what was behind the sighs, where her pain rested, and why. I longed to tell her she could leave behind her lonely nights and empty days—I'd fill them with happy memories to replace the sad.

Before I uttered promises I wasn't sure I could keep, I had to know in my heart I was making them for the right reasons. As long as she had no choice but to be with me, I wouldn't know for certain. Once she was free to get on with the rest of her life, then we'd see if we fit as well as I believed we did at this moment.

Rebel shuddered and pulled the throw she'd taken from the bed over her shoulders, and then looked behind her, and our eyes met.

"Hi," she murmured.

"Can't sleep?"

She shook her head.

"You look cold. Come back and let me get you warm."

"I can't."

"Why ever not?" The violet-tinged silver rays of the moon shone on her, and in that still, quiet moment, I felt as though she was already saying goodbye. It nearly broke my heart to think it was forever.

"You're a good man, Edge. Both Tee-Tee and Casper said so. They also both warned me not to fuck things up with you."

I raised a brow, finding it surprising that either woman would express such a sentiment.

"The thing is, I will fuck it up."

"Not if you don't want to."

She shook her head. "I know myself. I always push away first."

"What if I don't let you?"

"You won't be able to stop me."

"Rebel." I reached my hand out to her. "Come back to bed."

To my relief, she did as I asked. I wrapped her in my arms, hoping that when this was all over, she would still be here.

"When are you leaving?" she whispered.

I'd been dreading the question and was surprised she hadn't asked before now. "Tomorrow night."

"I'm scared," she whispered.

"You have nothing to be afraid of. Casper and I will do our jobs, and then you'll be free of all this." That's what I told her; however, inside I was scared too.

Since Sunday was the only day the dining hall was closed, with the exception of branding and calving season when there were times it was open all day and night for several days straight, I let Rebel sleep in.

I'd gotten up around eight to get a workout in. Periodically, I'd take a break and check on her, opening and closing the door as quietly as I could.

At noon, I received a text from Grinder asking when I wanted him to send Kick over. I hadn't yet told Rebel she wouldn't be staying here alone while I was gone, and I wasn't sure how she would react.

I still wasn't thrilled about Kick being on her detail. The only explanation I could muster was that I wouldn't trust anyone with her safety more than myself. Jealousy might play a role in it too, but that was harder to admit.

As much as I hated doing it, I had to wake her. When I opened the door, though, she was resting on her elbows.

"Good afternoon, sweetness."

"Hi. I've been thinking about getting out of bed."

I smiled. "What have you come up with?"

"I won't if you crawl in next to me."

"Would that I could, but there's someone I need to introduce you to."

She sat up straighter. "Who?"

"His name is Kick. He'll be taking over as your custodian while I'm gone."

I waited while she processed what I'd just told her.

"Is that really necessary?"

"I'm afraid it is."

"Can't Tee-Tee do it?"

I scrubbed my face with my hand. "I'd prefer that actually, but there is the matter of your safety. While Decker has tightened security on the ranch, the fact that someone got to you once…" I shook my head. "I cannot risk it." My mobile buzzed, and I took it out of my pocket. There was a text from Rile saying Smoke had established our cover with the ABT.

"Is everything okay?" she asked.

"We've received confirmation from Smoke," I answered without thinking.

"Who is Smoke again?"

"He's with the CIA, but more and more, I think he operates independently. Right now, he's in Idaho, undercover with the Aryan Nation."

She shuddered. "Scary."

"Smoke or the job?"

"I was talking about the job, but is he scary?"

"You remember Hammer? Your attorney?"

"Yeah, he's scary. I never would've guessed he was a lawyer."

"Well, Smoke makes Hammer look like a primary school teacher."

She laughed.

"I like seeing you smile."

"I wish you didn't have to leave."

I felt the same way, but I had no choice. It was imperative we find not only Possum's killer, but who the group was that backed him. I couldn't trust anyone else; Rebel's life was dependent on the success of this mission.

Once I'd introduced Rebel to Kick and he'd dropped his bags in the guest bedroom, I excused myself to the office. There were three things I needed to take care of before Casper and I went undercover.

First, I rang Hammer, and when he answered, I took the piss out of him for being uncommunicative.

"Rebel isn't my only client, asshole," he fired back. "If I had anything to report, you would've heard from me." He went on to inform me that he and the sheriff were working together behind the scenes. "Mac hasn't been able to trace the gun back to anyone, which isn't surprising. He's also not done trying."

"Has he brought in a gunsmith?" I asked, not wanting to admit I'd completely forgotten about the planted gun.

"Of course he has, Edge."

I ended the call feeling like a wanker for questioning him the way I had. I definitely wasn't feeling myself, and given I was about to leave for one of the most important missions of my life, I had to get myself together.

I rolled my shoulders and rang Decker, who reported that the cowboy who had approached Rebel in the dining hall had seemingly vanished into thin air. He and Boon had questioned the other ranch hands extensively, but it seemed the guy was more of a drifter than someone who had ties to this area. His background check came up squeaky clean, both before he was hired and when Decker ran it again. Something that bothered both of us equally.

Finally, I sent a text to my brother. I hadn't heard from Lennox and had no idea how things had gone between him and Emerson. *Are you engaged to be married?*

Not officially, but Emerson has agreed to spend her life with me, he answered within a few seconds.

Rather than send another text, I rang him.

"It's good to hear from you, Keon."

"Congratulations. I mean that sincerely."

"I love her so much. I never thought feeling this way was possible."

Neither did I, and yet inside me, I felt a stirring. "How long was it before you knew? Really knew?"

"The night we met."

During my recovery from arm surgery, Lennox had admitted he first met Emerson years prior, in a bar in London. They'd spent one night together. She left the next morning before dawn without either of them knowing the other's last name. "Truly?"

"I spent a long time trying to convince myself otherwise, but when I woke that morning and she was gone, I felt a pain like none I'd known. My heart knew then that she was the woman for me, even if it took my brain far longer to catch up."

"I'm happy for you, brother."

"I hope this for you, Keon. Nothing beyond the life Emerson and I are about to make with each other would make me happier than seeing you find the love of your life."

What would Lennox say if I told him I believed I had? Would he scoff? He'd just said he knew Emerson was the woman for him after only one night.

"I hear you're headed into the ABT."

"How in the bloody hell do you know that?" Although as soon as I asked, I realized the answer.

"I haven't yet officially resigned from MI6."

"What are you waiting for?"

"Nothing, I suppose."

"Then, do it. Come join the Invincibles."

"I'll need to be based on the East Coast."

"As if anyone would care where you were based."

"Then, I guess it's done."

"When will you give Z your resignation?"

"I just hit send on the email I'd already drafted."

"Bravo, brother."

"Thanks."

"Godspeed, Lennox."

"Godspeed, Keon."

I ended the call no less worried about what I was about to undertake, but buoyed by my brother's news, both personal and professional.

When I came out of the office, I found Kick and Rebel seated at the breakfast bar, chatting. Was it really necessary that the two be so *amiable*?

"Rile was looking for you," he said when he saw me studying them.

"Was he here?" I asked, annoyed with his lack of detail.

"He called."

I inwardly growled and stalked back into the office. Rather than calling Rile, I rang Grinder.

"Isn't there anyone else we could put on Rebel's detail?" I asked before he could say as much as hello.

When he laughed, I wanted to reach through the mobile and throttle him.

"I'm not joking."

"Listen to yourself. It's gotten personal, Edge," he said, his voice turning serious. "Too personal."

"Sod off."

"You're falling in love with her."

"What's your point?"

"Maybe instead of questioning whether Kick should be on Rebel's detail, you should be questioning whether you're the right man for this op."

If anyone else had dared utter those words to me, I wouldn't have accepted it. Grinder was different. He was my best mate, and if anyone could shake some sense into me, he could.

"You still there?" he asked.

"Yes, and you're right."

"What are you going to do about it?"

"Get my bloody head back on straight."

"You best. By the way, Decker needs to talk to you."

I heard a rustling sound and then Decker's voice on the line.

"Listen, I've got eyes and ears in place, but I need you to activate them."

"Since when do they need to be activated?"

"Since I fucked up."

It was unusual for Decker to make a mistake, and even rarer for him to admit it. I had no idea what to say.

"Look, Edge, this isn't an excuse, but…Mila's pregnant."

Unsure what to say, I congratulated him.

"Thanks. She's been sick almost around the clock."

I supposed that in the next few years, more and more of the men and women I worked with would be starting families. However, that likelihood didn't make me feel any better about the state of this op.

25

Rebel

I tried to pay attention to what this guy—Kick—
was saying, but as I watched the minutes on the clock
tick by, I knew that, at any moment, Edge would tell
me it was time for him to leave.

If only I could rewind the clock and take the night
off when my mom overdosed. She and I would've been
out for dinner or watching a movie or any other seemingly mundane thing, and Possum wouldn't have been
able to get to her. She'd still be alive, I wouldn't be
out on bail after being charged with murder, and Edge
wouldn't be about to risk his life for me. In fact, he'd
probably still be unaware of my existence.

I hadn't been able to sleep last night, knowing the
danger he was putting himself in because of me. I even
considered telling him I didn't care who murdered
Possum. I'd wanted to, wasn't that enough? What if I

told him I'd rather spend my life in jail than have anything happen to him?

I knew the answer. Nothing I said would change what Edge was about to do. He'd still do everything in his power, not only to exonerate me, but to save me from a life spent looking over my shoulder, knowing that, one day, whoever the Lynch guy was whose message was delivered by the ranch hand, would kill me.

When the office door opened and my eyes met his, I knew it was time.

"Would you excuse us?" he said to Kick, who immediately left us alone.

"I don't want you to do this," I blurted before Edge could say another word.

He rested his forehead against mine. "We both know I have to."

"I could…"

He shook his head without me finishing my sentence. "This is what we do, Rebel. We go in, and we get the bad guys."

"Please be careful."

"Always."

He kissed me—long and hard and deep. I wished we had more time, but even if we did, it would never be enough.

He cupped my cheek and looked into my eyes. "I'll be back as soon as I can."

I watched him walk out the door, praying he would be.

26

Edge

"Ready?" I asked Casper, who was standing by the window in Grinder's house. Her demeanor was as I expected it to be. She was calm and focused—ready to step into her role.

We had one more meeting with the team, and then we'd head out.

"Ready?" Grinder asked me like I'd just asked Casper.

I nodded, also like she had.

"How's the hand?"

I hated that he asked, but he was the only one from whom I'd accept the question. "Strong."

While Rile didn't ask about the strength of my hand, he grasped it in a firm handshake.

"Let's get on with it," I said to him, anxious to get through the briefing so we could be on our way.

Decker handed us ID cards. "Your cover is Colonel Jeremy Swift, an emissary sent by the AN. Casper, your cover is Cynthia Brand, former captain in the

WAU—Women for Aryan Unity—and Swift's common-law wife."

"Rile, can we run through the objectives in order of priority one more time?" Casper asked.

"Primary: identifying or getting the ABT to give up Possum's killer. Secondary: identifying the splinter group."

"There's one more," I said. "My guess is the Lynch guy is part of the splinter group. If not, we also need to either identify him or get the ABT to."

"Any other questions?" Rile asked.

"Negative," answered Casper.

"Jagger and Rage are on their way here now with your ride," Grinder announced.

"What's their twenty?"

"Just came in the gate," answered Decker, monitoring something on his laptop. "By the way, I was able to activate the audio and video feeds."

I didn't bother asking how. One, I didn't care as long as they were hot. Two, even if he had explained, I wouldn't have understood. Decker was a technological mastermind, probably the best in the world, not that he'd accept that title.

I saw the big black SUV pull up. The windows were the same dark color as the vehicle. "Armored?" I asked.

"A colonel in the Aryan Nation wouldn't travel any other way," murmured Rile. My eyes met Grinder's. We were used to the eldest partner in the Invincibles commenting unnecessarily, as though he was teaching *us* something. *The wanker.*

"I want you in and out in forty-eight hours or less," he added.

"Roger that," I muttered as Decker approached and handed me something flesh-colored and not much bigger than the head of a pin. "What is this?"

"Put it on the tip of your finger and then insert it as far as you can into your auditory canal."

"Are you fucking kidding me?" I exclaimed when I heard Grinder's voice slowly counting inside my head.

"Bloody brilliant, isn't it?" I heard him respond.

"Where are you?"

"Look out the window."

Grinder was standing in the driveway; there was no way he would've been able to hear me except through the thing I'd just inserted in my ear.

"The active charge life is seventy-two hours, give or take," said Decker, handing Casper the same thing he'd given me. "After which, we'll still be able to hear and see what is happening in the compound, at least in the main buildings. We won't have any means to communicate directly with you, however."

"Can you hear me?" Grinder asked through the device.

"Affirmative," answered Casper. I heard both his question and her response directly in my ear.

"Seventy-two hours," Decker repeated.

I planned to be out long before then. If we weren't, it would mean our problems were bigger than the charge life.

It took us less than thirty minutes to reach the ABT compound. It was nestled deep in the hills of North Austin, not far from the Central Texas Correctional Compound, and much too close to the ranch—and Rebel—for my comfort.

"Identification," the guard barked when I pulled up and lowered the driver's side window partway. I handed him the credentials Decker had prepared.

The guard read them and looked up at me with wide eyes. "Welcome to the ABT compound, sir." Then he looked beyond me at Casper. "Ma'am."

I raised the window without responding and pulled through the now-open gate. As I'd anticipated, several of the rank-and-file members were emptying out of the main building and stood at mock attention, awaiting our exit from the vehicle.

One man approached as I walked around to open the passenger door.

"Welcome, sir. We've been expecting you."

"Brecht?" He was the highest-ranking leader of the Texas group, and the great-grandson of the Nation's founder. The brief I'd read said he was jockeying for a promotion to the main compound located in Coeur d'Alene, Idaho. It was the main reason Smoke believed we'd be successful in getting him to give up Possum's killer.

"That's correct, sir."

I shook his extended hand, and he turned toward the men assembled.

"This is Colonel Swift. He's been sent here by the general. I expect each of you to treat him with due respect and cooperate with whatever he asks of you."

Several of them murmured their agreement; most remained silent. I was confident Casper was assessing the group in the same way I was. Most important was to identify those who appeared uninformed in advance of the visit. They were the contingent Brecht didn't trust.

"I'm here to observe as well as review your reports in advance of the World Congress," I announced. The annual meeting was scheduled to take place in three months' time in Idaho. Promotions, like the one Brecht was after, would be handed out at that meeting.

If the alleged splinter group was successful in either breaking off or in taking over the leadership of this chapter, Brecht would be held responsible. He would benefit from their being stopped more than anyone else, and I intended to exploit his ambition.

A few minutes later, Brecht escorted Casper and me to the compound's guesthouse reserved for VIPs.

In anticipation of our quarters being bugged, Decker had supplied us with jamming equipment that would block every signal but his. He would, of course, test it via the other technology he'd somehow put into place.

It wouldn't come as a surprise to whomever the ABT had monitoring us. Given who they believed we were, they would anticipate we'd seek out listening devices and disable them. Not doing so would immediately raise suspicion.

There was a mandatory dinner to welcome us held that evening. Casper knew to interact only with the other women present in an organization as misogynistic as this while I continued to play the role of a displeased high-ranking guest.

Once dinner was over, I was scheduled to meet with Brecht alone. Before I could do so, I was intercepted.

"Care for a smoke?" a man said as I was exiting the main dining hall.

"Ask if he has more than one," I heard Decker's voice say in my ear, and I did.

The man nodded and held up three fingers before walking away.

"What are they doing here?" I asked.

"I don't know, but I'm about to find out," Deck responded.

When I heard Casper ask one of the women where the bathroom was, I went around the side of the building and waited. Seconds later, she came out of the front door.

"Interesting development," she whispered.

Yeah, interesting wouldn't be the word I'd use. Why weren't we informed in advance that the FBI already had three agents on premises?

27

Rebel

Edge had been gone for almost forty-eight hours, and according to Kick, there was "nothing to report." I doubted he'd tell me if there was.

I spent most of my time the day before at the dining hall. At least there, I had something to keep me busy. I knew Tee-Tee sensed something was up with me, and thankfully, she hadn't asked what it was. I was a shitty liar, especially with her.

The other benefit of being at the dining hall was that Kick pretty much left me alone. As long as I let him drive me here in the morning and pick me up at the end of the day, he didn't hover.

Seeing it was a nice day, I decided to go outside to take a break between lunch and dinner. Right before I rounded the corner to exit through the back door, I heard voices coming from the storeroom.

"It's goin' down tonight," a voice that sounded a lot like that of the guy who'd threatened me said.

"Why are they advancing now?" I couldn't place the second voice, but whoever it was, was a male with a Hispanic accent.

"Big guns arrived from headquarters. It's now or never."

"Are you planning on taking out whoever the Nation sent in?"

"What choice do we have?"

"I'm out."

"You don't get 'out.' Once you're in, you're in, *cabrón.*"

As quietly as I could, I ran back through the kitchen. Once I was far enough away, I called Kick.

"You ready?" he asked, sounding sleepy. "I thought you were—"

"Get your ass here right now. It's an emergency," I whispered.

I heard him swear as I ended the call, but I didn't give a shit. He wanted to give me a hard time, I'd go above his head. The next person I called was Grinder.

"Fuck," I muttered when the call went straight to voicemail. I didn't have Rile's number. The only other person besides Tee-Tee that Edge had programmed in was Shadow, and I wasn't sure what her deal was. I remembered she mentioned the Invincibles the day she gave me all the clothes, but how much did she actually know about what they did?

When I saw Kick pull up, I ran out and climbed in the truck. "I overheard two men talking about something going down tonight at the ABT. They said they were going to take out the people the Aryan Nation sent in." I expected him to throw the truck into gear and head to wherever the rest of the Invincible team were. Instead, he just sat there. *"What the fuck are you waiting for?"*

I looked in the same direction as Kick and saw the asshole who'd threatened me headed in our direction. I jumped out of the truck, and when Kick came after me, I didn't stop to think; I shot the motherfucker, and when he dropped, I raced back to the truck, threw it into gear, and punched it.

By the time the other asshole realized what was happening and raised his gun, I was close enough to plow straight for him, firing through the passenger window. I hit him and he went down, but I didn't have time to stop and make sure he was dead. If he wasn't, he was pretty fucking close.

28

Edge

"I didn't copy. Repeat."

"I said Rebel is less than ten minutes from the gate of the compound, and she's armed."

"What the fuck?" Casper mouthed.

"Kill the fucking truck! Stop her!" Every one of our vehicles had a remote kill switch. Decker had installed them himself. I didn't understand what he was waiting for.

"If I do that, she'll be a sitting duck. She's too close."

"Jesus Christ, Decker. What the fuck is going on?"

Casper motioned for me to lower my voice.

"We're on our way, but we aren't going to make it in time to intercept her."

"Why is she headed here?" Casper asked.

"We think she may have intercepted a message at the same time we did, about something going down at the compound tonight. Grinder's phone registered a call from her, but we were already mobilizing. She got at least a ten-minute head start on us."

"What's going down, Decker?" Casper pushed when I didn't.

"Chatter that the splinter group is staging a coup. Both you and Edge are included in the target list."

"Have you identified any members of the group?" I asked.

"Negative. Our only goal now is to get you and Casper out."

"Roger that. We're headed to the gate." I pulled out my gun at the same time I heard one cock, and it wasn't Casper's.

"Where y'all goin' in such a hurry?" asked Brecht, standing in the doorway with his gun leveled at me. "Drop it or I'll end him," he said when Casper raised hers at him. "You too," he said to me.

"Tell him," I heard Decker say.

"You've got a splinter group ready to stage a coup. That's why we're here."

"Who the hell are you, and don't fucking try to tell me you're with the Nation."

"He's with the FBI," said the man who'd offered me the smoke as he came around the corner. "Ain't that right?"

The agent's words distracted Brecht long enough that I could get a shot off from the other gun he didn't know I had. I hit him square in the chest.

"Head out," the agent said. "We'll take it from here."

I had a split second to decide. If this mission ended, it would all be for nothing. We still hadn't managed to get Brecht to give up Possum's killer, and now he was dead.

"Go," I told Casper, who'd heard everything I had. "Intercept Rebel."

"How far out is she now, Deck?" she asked.

"Five."

"Kill the goddamn truck, Decker."

"Edge—"

"Right fucking now!"

29

Rebel

"What the—" I lurched as the old pickup screeched to a dead stop. If I had been going any faster, the fucking thing would've flipped. I tried to restart it and got nothing. *Nothing.* It was as though the engine, the starter, the whole damn truck had been zapped dead.

I'd just popped the hood when I saw a big black SUV hurtling my way. I grabbed my gun and was about to fire when it pulled up beside me and I saw it was Casper driving.

"Get in!" she shouted, motioning with her head to the back passenger door. I was barely in the back seat when she punched the SUV in the direction I'd come from.

"Turn around! We have to go back!" I screamed at her. *"They're gonna kill Edge!"*

She kept going as though she hadn't heard me.

"You're in on it," I muttered, reaching for my gun.

"Don't even fucking think about it," she seethed. "And I'm not in on anything. In fact, Edge is back there alone because I had to come out and save your ass."

She slammed on the brakes when another SUV approached from the opposite direction. Behind that one were two more.

"What's going on?"

She ignored me and rolled down the window. "I'm going back in. It looked like some kind of raid was taking place when I left," she told Grinder, who was driving the first SUV. "You get her out of here."

"Negative. She'll go back with Quint and Shadow."

"Where the fuck are they?" Casper yelled.

"Third vehicle back," he said before he sped off. The second SUV went by just as fast. The third stopped.

"Get out," Casper spat.

"No. Take me in with you."

She spun around and grabbed me by the collar of my shirt. "Listen to me. Because of *you* and your reckless behavior, Edge is in even more danger. Get the fuck out *now!*"

"I've got this," said Shadow, opening the back door. "Come with me, Rebel. Let the agents finish this."

What choice did I have? I got out and went with Shadow.

"You've been busy," Shadow said when she climbed in the back seat with me. "Let's see, two men down, one a federal agent, I might add. You better hope he pulls through, or that will really cost you."

30

Edge

"We're headed your way," Grinder said through the earpiece. "Shadow has Rebel. She's safe and being transported back to the ranch. What's it look like inside? Casper said something about a raid."

"It's mostly over; Brecht is down. It's complicated, but according to the feds, he was the one who carried out the hit on Possum."

"I didn't copy. Repeat."

"I'll explain when you get in here, but you can stand down." What neither Casper nor I realized when Brecht confronted us on our way to leave was, at that same time, the FBI had descended on the compound in a full-stop raid. Agents had stormed the place en masse, coming in from every direction. It had to have been planned for days if not weeks—which begged the question: why hadn't we been briefed on what was already in place within the ABT? Smoke had to have known about it.

I saw the first of our SUVs pull in from where I stood inside the main building, watching as the FBI systematically took the members of the Aryan Brotherhood of Texas into custody, charging them with illegal weapon possession along with a myriad of other things.

"Would've been nice for them to tell us about this. I could've finished my pint," said Grinder as he and Decker got out. A few seconds later, another SUV pulled up; Rile, Jagger, and Rage exited that one, followed shortly thereafter by Casper. While my teammates surveyed the scene taking place, I walked over to the man who'd initially made contact with me, John McIntyre, code name Trapper. "Anyone named Lynch been processed yet?"

He scanned the list. "Negative."

"Let me know if that changes."

"It won't. We're through everyone."

"You're certain?"

When he glared at me, I walked back over to where the Invincibles team stood waiting.

"You don't look happy."

"We failed one of our objectives."

Rile shook his head. "The feds confirmed Brecht killed Possum, as well as determined which members were part of the splinter group. Not that it matters." He waved his hand. "The ABT is finished."

He was right. One of the things I'd learned in our two days here was that the Texas organization was low on manpower as well as funds. It wasn't just the splinter group who was unhappy with Brecht; many of the other members were equally concerned about the Texas chapter's future.

"McIntyre said there's no Lynch on the list of arrests."

Rile brushed his lower lip with the tip of his index finger. "That is concerning. Could it be Rebel misheard the name?"

"Speaking of Rebel," said Grinder, "she tried to kill Kick."

"Bloody hell." I scrubbed my face with my hand. "Are you serious?"

"I think he's going to pull through."

Something else occurred to me, and I looked at Rile. "Was he a fed?"

The man slowly nodded.

"You goddamn wanker—"

Grinder stepped in front of me. "This will all come out in the hotwash, Edge. This is neither the time nor the place."

I stood down but pointed my finger in Rile's direction. "You better have a fucking good reason why you kept Casper and me in the dark about this."

Grinder remained between Rile and me. "I don't think there's much more we can do here, Edge. You ready to roll?"

The idea that we still hadn't identified the name referenced when the ranch hand threatened Rebel plagued me. I doubted she misheard, as Rile had suggested she might have.

"Ride back with Casper and me. You can brief me on what went down with Rebel."

Grinder nodded and handed the key fob to Decker.

"Go on," said Rile to Jagger and Rage. "I'm going to stay and see what else I can find out."

I turned away from him, still bloody pissed off that he would withhold information from me.

"Edgemon?" he said, motioning me toward him. What I really wanted to do was flip him off, but I stopped myself from doing so.

"What?"

"I was not aware of the FBI's involvement. I was also unaware of Kick's affiliation with them. He came to us through Smoke, whose word I trusted—perhaps until now."

I looked into his eyes and knew he was being honest with me. Rile was not the type of man to shirk responsibility. If he'd done what I accused him of, he would've admitted it while, at the same time, defending why he had.

"Understood."

"Edge?"

"We're good, Rile."

He nodded and I walked away.

Casper drove while Grinder briefed me on everything he knew about what had gone down with Rebel, which wasn't much.

I sent a text to Shadow, who confirmed Rebel was at the main residence with her and Quint.

When I walked inside, Rebel jumped up from where she was waiting at the table and ran over to me.

"Thank God you're okay," she said, rushing into my open arms.

"It's over, sweetness." The words were out before I realized that wasn't exactly true. It wasn't over. There was still the question of who the hell Lynch was. "We have a lot to talk about," I said, brushing her hair from her face.

"You need to hear my side of the story," she said, looking over her shoulder at where Shadow remained seated.

"And I shall."

"Can we go back to the house now?"

"Of course." I waved in Shadow's direction, and she gave me the okay sign before waving back.

We were both quiet on our way to the house. So much had happened in the last forty-eight hours, it was almost inconceivable. What we needed more than anything was rest.

"What happens now?" Rebel asked when we walked into the kitchen. I wasn't sure where to begin to answer that question. Next with what?

"As far as the charges against you, I would imagine there will be a hearing tomorrow. If not then, soon. After which, you'll be free."

"Then what?"

"The bail money will be refunded, and we can move on with our lives. I don't know about you, but I have some ideas about what I'd like to do."

She cocked her head. "What?"

"Take some time off—something I never do—and go hang out for a month or two at a beachfront villa somewhere, the kind that wouldn't require we wear clothes—"

Rebel's mouth dropped open, and she gaped at me. "What?"

"Are you serious?"

"To a certain extent. I mean, that was off the cuff, but after saying it out loud, it sounds pretty nice." Especially considering we didn't have a lead on Lynch. It would give the team time to find him while I kept Rebel safe.

She turned her back and put her hand on her stomach.

I tried to put my arm around her waist, but she spun away from me. "Talk to me, Rebel. Tell me what you're thinking."

31

Rebel

I was having trouble sorting everything going through my head. "I need some time to myself." I started down the hallway, but Edge followed. "Did you not hear me?"

"I did, but no, I'm not giving you time to yourself. Tell me what the hell I said wrong."

I took several deep breaths, not that doing so was helping me settle down any. Edge's offhanded way of dismissing the shitstorm my life had been for the last several weeks, struck a chord somewhere deep inside me. While the murder charge would be dropped, what I'd lost because of it wouldn't miraculously reappear.

I had nowhere to live, and I'd probably lose my job since I'd no longer be staying on the ranch. I had no money. *None.*

Edge stood in front of me and dropped his hands to his sides. "Do you want to explain why you're so angry?"

"I don't know where to begin."

"Why don't we go lie down, and you can tell me what's on your mind." He reached for me, but I backed away.

"No."

"Rebel, for God's sake, after what I've been through—what we've been through—can we please just get some rest and discuss this in the morning?"

"Sure," I said, but I didn't go into the master bedroom. I opened the door to the guest room, relieved to see that Kick's stuff was gone. That was another thing we needed to talk about. Evidently, I'd shot and almost killed a federal agent, but I was still convinced he'd been in on whatever the two men I'd overheard talking in the storeroom were involved in.

"What are you doing?" he asked when I stood in the doorway.

"Getting some rest."

"Not in there, you're not." He grabbed my arm. *Bad move.* I wrenched it away. When he stepped forward, I took another step back. I was about to close the door on him, but he was too quick. He reached behind my knees, scooped me up, and carried me into his bedroom. Unlike the other times he'd done the same thing, this time it felt controlling, like I was his fucking prisoner.

When he put me down on the bed, I got right back up and stalked toward the door.

"Rebel!" he shouted at me. *"Stop this ridiculousness. I'm too exhausted to deal—"*

Before he could finish his sentence, I slammed the door and walked out. Once I got to the guest room, I slammed that door too and locked it.

I sat on the bed and put my head in my hands. Edge wanted me to explain why I was so angry, but I couldn't. Even I didn't know why I'd initially reacted the way I had. All I knew now was that I needed to be alone.

The next morning, when I came out of the bedroom after getting very little sleep, Edge was sitting on the sofa.

"We need to talk." He pointed to the chair. "Have a seat." When I sat in a different chair, he laughed.

"Do you think I'm funny?"

He leaned forward and rested his elbows on his knees. "No, Rebel. I don't, but I do think you're behaving childishly."

"Fuck you." I stood and he did too.

"We're going to talk, one way or another."

"What is that supposed to mean?"

"It means you are going to sit down, shut up, and listen to what I have to say."

"Or?"

"Or you can leave."

"Perfect. That's exactly what I intend to do." I stalked back to the master bedroom, shoved my photos in one of my boxes, picked it up, and carried it into the kitchen.

"What are you doing?"

"Leaving, like you told me I had to."

"You can't."

"Watch me." I stalked back into the bedroom, grabbed the other box, and carried it out. "Please give me my car keys."

Edge shook his head. "You can't leave until after the hearing."

"Tell you what. I'll drive from here straight to the sheriff's office. If he wants to put me in jail until the hearing, I'm fine with that."

"You'd rather go back to jail than talk to me?"

"Damn straight. It's what I've wanted since you bailed me out."

I watched as he clenched and unclenched his fists and then reached behind and rubbed the back of his neck. "Please, Rebel. Let's just talk. I'm begging here."

I set the box on the floor and folded my arms.

"Can we sit? Please?"

"Sure." I walked back over to the chair I'd been sitting in before, plopped myself down, and waited.

"Somehow, things went terribly wrong last night. I'm still unsure of exactly what I said that set you off, but whatever it was, I'm sorry."

He looked at me as though he expected me to say something. I had nothing.

"Was it that I suggested we go away?"

I looked out the window. "In part."

"Explain why."

"You may be independently wealthy, Edge, but after everything I've told you, how could you assume I was?"

"I didn't assume anything of the kind. I've told you time and time again that the money doesn't matter to me. I *thought* that, after what you've been through, you'd appreciate getting away for a while."

"Just like that? The murder charge is dropped, and suddenly, I go 'back' to living my fancy life?"

"You've nothing to worry about any longer, Rebel. You're free."

"Nothing to worry about? I still don't have any money, even though you said I'll get paid for my job at the dining hall. I don't even know if my car runs, and I have no place to live."

"You can stay here."

"*Stay* here? As what, Edge? Your lover?"

"For now."

"As in, I can stay here until I get back on my feet?" I shook my head. He was so far out of touch with *my* reality, I wondered why I was even trying to explain my feelings to him.

"If you want to look at it that way. How many times do I have to repeat that I don't care about the money?"

"What if I care about it?" Did he think I had no pride at all?

"I don't know what else to say to get through to you, Rebel. You've no reason to worry about things between you and me."

"Until you're done 'taking care of me.' What happens then?"

"I don't know. We'll figure something out."

We'll figure something out? It may be that simple for him, but I'd already lost almost four months of my life, more if I was honest.

From the time my mother overdosed until now, I'd been going through the motions. I'd put one foot in front of the other, but I wasn't really living. Had I ever done more with my life than exist paycheck to paycheck in a crappy job? The most money I'd ever made was as a bartender. Edge was suggesting that we go away for a month or two, come back and then, again, figure something out. My life would never be so carefree or simple.

It was pointless to even try to discuss this with him. It was obvious he didn't understand, and that meant he couldn't relate to the kind of life I lived and likely never would. I had to get out of here. "Where are Susan's keys?"

"Your car?"

"Yes. My car. Where are my car keys?"

"I have them. Why?"

"Can you please give them to me?" I stood and held my hand out. "Just give me my fucking keys, and you'll never have to see me again."

"What about your job with Tee-Tee?"

"You're concerned about that now? Last night, you had me taking 'a month or two' off like it was nothing."

"We certainly would've discussed it with her."

I closed my eyes and counted to five. It didn't help. When I opened them again, the expression on Edge's face almost made me give in. He looked sad. Really sad. Devastated sad.

"Look, I really appreciate everything you've done for me. I don't know where to begin to repay you for your kindness and generosity. But…you and I are nothing alike. We have nothing in common, and I have no clue how to make my way in your world. What's more, I don't want to. I'm my own person, Edge. I'm independent. I rely on myself and no one else. Like I said, I don't know how to repay you, but I will. Somehow, I'll repay every penny you spent on me."

"I don't want you to repay me."

I shook my head. He wasn't even listening to me. Once again, he was focused solely on money. This was about so much more than that. "I need to go. I can't stay here, Edge. If I have to, I'll walk, but I'd much rather you just give me the keys to my car."

He stood, walked into the kitchen, opened a drawer, and pulled them out. "Here."

"Thanks." I grabbed them, picked up a box, and took it out to my car. When I turned to go back inside for the other, Edge was behind me with it in his arms. He set it in my trunk and slowly walked over and opened the garage door.

"Rebel?"

I had my hand on the car door. "What?"

"Do you have your mobile with you?"

My cheeks burned. "I forgot. I'm sorry." I pulled it out and walked over to hand it to him.

"No. I want you to keep it. I want you to be able to reach me."

I sighed, knowing that, as it was with so many other things, I didn't have a choice. I'd need some way to communicate with Tee-Tee and maybe even the sheriff. "I'll return it as soon as I get another one."

"I wish you wouldn't do this."

"I have to, Edge. I can't stay here."

He closed his eyes and nodded. "Be safe, Rebel."

"I will."

"If you need anything—anything at all—please come to me, call me."

"I can take the clothes back to Shadow if you want me to."

He shook his head. "She said they're yours to keep."

"I don't want them."

"I'll take care of it."

"Thank you. Thank you for everything." Before I burst into tears, which I was close to doing, I got in the car and put the key in the ignition. I had no idea if it would start. If it didn't, it would make this whole overly dramatic exit pretty lame.

It started, thank God. I backed out of the garage, not allowing myself to look to see if Edge was still standing in it or if he'd gone inside. If I did, I might lose my resolve.

I parked Susan near the dining hall and walked up to the door. Like whether my car would start or not, I wondered if I'd still have access to this building. When I put my palm on the pad and looked into the reader, the door clicked open.

Tee-Tee was sitting at the desk in the kitchen but stood and rushed over to me. "*Mija?* What are you doing here? I heard what happened yesterday. *¡Ay, Dios mio!*" She crossed herself.

"I need to talk to you, Tee-Tee."

"Come and sit." She led me to where she'd been sitting and pulled another chair over. "Tell me what happened."

God, I was going to miss this woman. Being around her after so many years, even for a short while, had been so comforting. She was the mother I wished I had. Loving, direct, tough as nails. I could add forgiving and generous now too. Although she'd always been generous. Even when she had little to nothing, she shared what she had. That was how I met her after all, when Blanca shared her lunch with me.

"I want you to know how much I appreciate the chance you gave me…" I blew out a deep breath, trying my damndest not to cry. "I've never been so appreciative of anyone in my life. Just that you believed I could do it meant more than anything."

"You're not telling me what happened. It sounds like you're saying goodbye. Why?"

My shoulders slumped forward. "Because I am."

"I don't understand."

"The murder charges against me are going to be dropped. It might happen as soon as today. I won't be living on the ranch any longer."

"I'm very happy to hear that, but it doesn't answer my question about why you're leaving."

"Edge has been so kind, so generous, but I can't take advantage of him any longer. I'm sure when he agreed to be my custodian, he didn't realize what he was getting himself into."

"What I don't understand is why you're leaving your job here."

"I just told you, I won't be living on the ranch."

"So?"

"You gave me this job as a favor to Edge. Don't try to deny it, Tee-Tee."

"Maybe, but you earned the chance to stay."

Argh. I didn't want to get angry with Tee-Tee, but she wasn't even trying to understand my situation. She, of all people, should understand how difficult the next few months would be for me. Her life had been damn hard at one time too—I'd seen it firsthand.

"I don't like this, Lucy."

"If you think I won't pay him back, you're wrong. It isn't like I'm just going to walk away and not pay him back for all the expenses he incurred on my behalf. I will as soon as I can find a job and get back on my feet."

"Where will you live?"

I hadn't gotten that far. My car would probably have to double as my home until I could save enough money to get a place.

Before I could come up with an answer, she stood. "You'll live with me."

I stood too. "What? No. I can't do that. I appreciate it so much, though. I can't tell you how much."

"No arguments. You're living with me."

"Tee-Tee—"

"No, not Tee-Tee, *Tía.* You'll show me the proper respect."

I smiled. "*Tía,* I truly appreciate what you're trying to do, but—"

"*¡Siéntate!*" she shouted and then softened her tone. "There's something I need to say."

I sat down like she told me to, and she did too.

"I owe you an apology. It's something I'm ashamed it's taken me this long to do."

"*Tía,* you don't have to do this—"

"*¡Silencio!*"

I folded my hands in my lap. "Go ahead."

"I accused you of something you didn't do, because I didn't want to believe what was right in front of my eyes. Blanca…" Tee-Tee stopped talking and crossed herself. "She was my baby girl. I didn't want to believe…maybe if I had, she'd still be alive."

I reached over and covered her hand with mine.

"You didn't steal that money. I know that now. I knew it then, if I had been strong enough to be honest with myself. I'm sorry."

"It's okay."

"It isn't 'okay.' Do you accept my apology or not?"

I smiled again. "I accept your apology."

"Good. Then you'll let me make it up to you. You'll come and live with me."

"That was a dirty trick."

She leaned forward, got right in my face, and scrunched her eyes. "If you don't live with me, I'll tell Edge you're living on the street. He'll find you, you know."

"What makes you think I'll be living on the street?"

"Because you have nowhere else to go."

We had a stare-down until I finally blinked. "If I do this, I'm going to have stipulations."

Tee-Tee smiled. "Always the rebel."

"I'm serious."

"And I'm listening."

"I'm paying rent."

"Yes. You are. What else?"

"Edge can't know."

"That one's more difficult."

"Why?"

"Because he used to be a spy, *Mija.* I think he still might be."

I patted her hand. "Yes. He still is. And if he finds out on his own, I can't do anything about that, but if he asks you, I want you to tell him that if he wants to know anything about me, to ask me himself."

Tee-Tee tapped her lower lip with her finger. "Okay. What else?"

"That's it. No, wait. How much am I getting paid?"

"Twenty-five dollars per hour."

"What? No. That's way too much."

"Twenty?"

"That's still a lot, Tee-Tee. I don't have any experience."

"*Tía,* and yes, you do. We work long hours here at the ranch, and the Alexander family pays us well. You'll be no exception. Quint will fire me if I underpay you."

I rolled my eyes. "Sure, he will."

"Then he'll give you my job. Is that what you want?"

I laughed, but she didn't look away. "Of course it isn't. Don't be silly."

"So, what are you waiting for? Hug me and then decide what you're making for dessert this week."

"You're a slave driver."

"Which is why I'm paying you so much money."

"I love you, *Tía.*"

"I love you too, *Mija.*"

"Oh! Where do you live?"

"Here on the ranch."

"I know that, but where on the ranch?"

"On the other side of the ranch manager's house."

I inwardly groaned. "The house Edge lives in?"

She winked. "That's right."

<h1 style="text-align:center">32</h1>

Edge

Grinder set his beer on the breakfast bar. "She just left?"

I took a swig and set mine down too. "Asked for her car keys and drove away."

"Just like that?"

I sighed. "As I said…yes."

"What did you do?"

"Drank a couple of pints and then rang you."

"No. What did you do to make her leave?"

"Thanks a lot, mate. You can sod right off."

"She wouldn't have left with no reason, Edge. Even you would have to admit that. Walk me through it."

I pulled another beer from the fridge and sat next to him. "If you want another, you can get it yourself."

"Wanker," he muttered, standing. "Talk," he said when he sat back down.

"She asked what would happen next, and I told her there'd likely be a hearing to officially drop the charges against her."

"That's it?"

"Pretty much."

Grinder shook his head. "What else, Edge. Come on, fess up."

"I suggested we take a vacation to celebrate."

"You didn't?"

"What of it?"

"You're a bloody idiot." Grinder got up from his stool and walked over to the window.

"What is so wrong with a vacation? I thought I was being nice."

"What about her job at the dining hall?"

"I told her we'd talk to Tee-Tee about it."

"Is it your job now?"

I walked over to where he stood. "I'll say it again. I was trying to be nice."

"Right, but you failed miserably. Is she a puppy? You'll keep her fed and watered, take her out to play?"

"It isn't like that."

"No? Unless you're leaving a lot out, that's how it seems to me. Did you even ask what *she* wanted?" Grinder pointed to something outside; I followed his line of sight. "At least she'll be close by."

I watched as Rebel carried her boxes from her car into the house Tee-Tee lived in, and waited for her to look this way. She didn't.

"Come on, then, Rile's pissing vinegar that we aren't over there yet."

I nodded and followed Grinder out, but not before I took one more look over my shoulder. Rebel was angry, but like the other times she was, she'd get over it. She might even be back later tonight.

When I rubbed my hands together in anticipation, Grinder shook his head. "Like I said, you're a bloody idiot."

By the time we finished the hotwash of the job, I was more bladdered than I had any business being. One thing continued to eat at me. *Lynch.* We still had no idea who he was.

"You stayed yesterday, Rile. Did anyone mention the name Lynch after I left?"

He shook his head. "No one affiliated with the ABT, past or present. As I said, could Rebel have heard the name wrong?"

It was possible, but since she wasn't speaking to me, I'd have to wait until tomorrow, or maybe longer, to ask. In fact, it was probably time I went home, just in case she showed up there. I had no idea what bloody time it even was. All I knew was it looked like it was getting dark.

I stood from the table and was about to walk out when Casper put her hand on my arm.

"Can I talk to you for a minute?"

"Always," I answered, draping my arm around her shoulders.

She waved her hand in front of her face. "You're drunk. Maybe I should wait until tomorrow."

"I'm not that drunk."

Casper laughed. "You are."

"Come on, what did you want to talk to me about?"

"I was wondering…I heard Rebel left, so…I thought maybe, if you wouldn't mind…maybe, could I stay with you for a couple of days?"

"Uh, okay. I mean, yes. Of course you can. Can I ask why?"

"I'm thinking about giving up my place in Florida. It's hard, ya know?"

"I do know." I shook my head, more to clear my thoughts. I was handling this badly and only because

I had a few too many pints. "I was just about to walk over. Come with me?"

"Thanks, Edge. I really appreciate this." She kissed my cheek. "I have to talk to Rile, but after I do, I'll grab my stuff and meet you over there."

With every step I took from Grinder's place to mine, the feeling that this was a terrible decision grew stronger.

I'd never thought much about window coverings until Grinder mentioned not wanting to see me starkers, but with Casper staying here for a couple of days and Rebel staying over at Tee-Tee's, I wished I could put draperies over them all.

Was it even close enough that she'd be able to see into the house? I thought briefly about running over to check how much could be seen from there. *Terrible idea.* What if Tee-Tee shot me for trespassing? Blimey, what a stupid thought that was. Why had I gotten so pissed? What I needed right now was a clear mind, and mine was bloody foggy.

A few minutes later, I heard a knock at the door. I scrubbed my face with my hand and went around the corner to open it, never expecting that instead of Casper, Rebel would be standing on the threshold.

"Can we talk?"

"Uh…sure, sure. Come in." I looked beyond her for Casper, but it was too dark to see.

"Expecting someone else?"

"Uh…no, no." Why was I lying to her when Casper would be here at any moment?

"You sure about that?"

I scrubbed my face a second time, again wishing I wasn't so pissed.

"Can I get you anything?"

"A beer would be nice. Thanks."

I opened the fridge and pulled out a bottle. "Glass?"

"I'm good. Not having one?"

"Nah. I've had a few already."

"So…I want to apologize for the way I left this morning."

I couldn't focus on what she was saying as I waited with dread for another knock on the door. "Accepted."

"Edge? Is everything okay?"

"Yeah, yeah. Why?"

"First of all, why do you keep repeating everything twice? 'Sure, sure.' 'No, no.' 'Yeah, yeah.'"

I scrubbed my face a third time. "Long day, I guess."

"And you keep rubbing your hand over your face."

"Listen, the truth is—"

Knock, knock.

"I thought you weren't expecting anyone."

"It's just Casper. You know, about the job." I walked around the corner and over to the front door, hoping she'd just go along with everything I said when she saw Rebel sitting in the kitchen. Before I could utter a syllable, I watched as one sentence unraveled any progress I'd momentarily hoped to make.

"Thanks again for letting me stay, Edge. I can't say I'm sorry Rebel left."

I took Casper by the arm. "And, as you can see, she's back." Probably not my most eloquent attempt at salvaging anything at all with the woman I wished had come back to stay forever.

"I was just leaving." Rebel slammed past me and out the front door, closing it so hard I thought the paintings might fall from the walls.

"Oh, no. God, Edge. I'm so sorry."

My eyes met Casper's. "It's okay." But it wasn't, and something told me it never would be again.

"Bloody hell," I groaned when I rolled over and the sun shone in my eyes. It wasn't so much that I was hungover; it was more the memory of how quickly my life had gone straight to hell that made me want to crawl into a cave. Or go lie on a beach for a month. Not without Rebel, though.

I picked up my mobile and checked the time. Half past nine, which meant I'd missed breakfast at the dining hall. It would be another ninety minutes before lunch service began and I'd have a chance to talk to Rebel.

Was going there even fair? But I had to. I couldn't ring her. When I talked to her, it had to be in person. Maybe it would be better if I showed up near the end of dinner and asked if we could talk after.

The idea of getting out of bed to take a shower felt like a punch to my gut. If I set foot in that bloody lavatory, all I'd see would be Rebel's unbearably hot body in the tub I prayed I'd talk her back into one day.

My phone chimed, but with an alert from Grinder, not Rebel. I thought about ignoring him, but given I'd slept most of the morning away, I decided against it.

Get your arse out of bed, you lazy wanker, the text read.

Sod off.

Let's ride.

If anything could get me out of bed, that was it. It had been too long since I'd ridden out. Maybe that's why my head was so far up my arse.

I managed to take a shower by averting my eyes from the tub. Thank God she and I hadn't shagged in there, or I might've had to resort to using the guest lav, or even go as far as to move out of this house altogether.

I was done for. Grinder was right, whether he was trying to take the piss out of me or not. I had fallen in love with Rebel, and I had to get her back. That was all there was to it.

"Good morning," said Casper when I walked down the hall and found her sitting at the breakfast bar. "I made coffee, but it's probably cold now."

"No worries." I walked over to the fridge, opened and shut it. "I'll get something at the barn."

"Listen, Edge, I want to apologize for what happened last night and also tell you I'm leaving."

I didn't know what to say. I wanted her to leave. "Oh?"

"With Christmas coming, I thought maybe it would be a good time to get my place ready to put on the market. A lot of people come to Florida in January."

"Right. Good idea."

"I really am sorry. I wish you'd at least look at me."

She was right. I hadn't. I turned around. "No need to be sorry. What happened was my fault. It started long before you arrived."

"But I made it worse."

I shook my head. "I feel like a bloody wanker now. You don't have to go…"

"Yeah, I do, Edge."

I noticed her bag was already by the door to the garage.

"I'm catching a ride to the airport with Rile."

"Good. That's good." I ran my hand through my hair, and she got off the stool and walked over to me.

"Thanks, Edge. Rile's here now."

We embraced, cheek-kissed, and she left. I wondered if I hadn't come out of the bedroom when I did, if I would've even known she was gone.

33

Rebel

I was standing in the kitchen, multiplying my recipe for bread pudding, when I heard the dining hall door open. I rested my hand on the gun tucked into the waistband of my pants, and leaned over to see who had come in. It didn't matter that Edge or anyone else told me the thing with Possum was over. Since the day I was threatened, I wore a gun everywhere I went.

"Fuck," I muttered when I saw Casper walk in. Too late to go hide in the storeroom and pretend I didn't see her.

She walked straight into the kitchen like she owned the place. Same way she'd walked into Edge's house last night.

"Can I help you?" I heard Tee-Tee ask from somewhere behind me.

"I'm here to see Rebel."

I set down my pencil and paper. "What do you want?" She smiled. Did she find me funny? Fuck her. I turned on my heel to walk away.

"Wait. I want to apologize."

I turned back around but stood where I was. If she wanted to say she was sorry, she could do it from ten feet away.

"I led you to believe that something had gone on between Edge and me. Nothing ever did."

"He told me."

"My husband died—"

"He told me that too."

"I guess you aren't gonna make this easy on me."

"Should I?"

She smiled again. "It's too bad things between us got off on the wrong foot. I like you, Rebel."

I couldn't say the same, but I was already being enough of a bitch. "Was there anything else?"

"Edge loves you."

I put my hand on my stomach and laughed. "Right. Edge loves me. That's a good one. Edge doesn't even know me."

"Well, that's all I came to say. I hope you'll give him another chance."

"Thanks." I watched her walk out, wishing I had it in me to be as big of a person as she was. When I looked over, Tee-Tee was studying me, maybe thinking the same thing. "Wait," I hollered after her.

Casper stopped walking and turned toward me.

"Two things. First, I'm really sorry about your husband, and second, thank you for everything you did for me. I guess I pretty much owe you my life."

She smiled again. "No, you owe your life to Edge."

She walked out, and I wanted to scream. Yes, I did owe Edge my life. Nice of her to fucking remind me.

"I need to go for a walk. I'll be back," I said to Tee-Tee from where I stood.

She didn't answer, but I was supposed to be on a break anyway. I made sure the car Casper got in drove away before I stormed out of the dining hall's front door and walked straight into Edge.

"Hey," he said, gripping my shoulders. "Where are you off to in such a hurry?"

I wiggled out of his grasp and took a step back. "For a walk."

"I was just about to go for a ride. Do you have time to join me?"

A ride sounded like the best thing ever. It had been so long since I was on horseback. I couldn't remember the last time. I looked over at the man standing a few feet away. Edge followed my gaze.

"Hi, Grinder."

He waved from where he stood. "Hey, Rebel."

"You two riding together?"

Grinder shook his head. "Actually, I was just headed back to the house."

He left, and Edge turned back to me. "So, what do you say about the ride?"

"I only have about an hour."

"We'll make it a short one, then."

"You just missed your friend."

"My friend?"

"Casper stopped by to talk to me."

"Oh."

"Don't worry," I said when I saw his furrowed brow. "She apologized for last night."

"Something I should do as well. I'm sorry, Rebel."

"I'm sorry too, Edge."

"Did she say anything else?"

"Not really." *Yes, as a matter of fact, she told me you loved me and that I owed you my life.* There was no way I was going to tell him either of those things.

When we walked into the barn, I was shocked to see Tee-Tee sitting in the office.

"Hi," I said, following Edge in.

"Nice walk?" She winked.

"We're going for a ride," Edge answered. "As long as it's okay with Boon if we take a couple of the horses out."

"*Mija,* have you met Boon?"

"At the dining hall."

"That's right. Well, have a nice ride."

"It'll be a short one. I'll be back in time for lunch."

"Take all the time you want. Lunch is ready. I don't need you today."

"*Tía…*" I gave her my sternest look.

"What? Do you think I'd be sitting around talking to Boon if lunch weren't ready? Have fun, *Mija.*"

We'd been out riding for maybe twenty minutes when Edge brought his horse to a stop.

"Rebel, I really am sorry."

"It's okay, Edge. I know you meant well."

"You do?"

"A little high-handed, but yeah."

He laughed when I did.

"I need to be serious for a minute, though. Okay?"

The smile left his face. "Of course."

"I know you think you know me, but the truth is, I don't even know myself. I stayed up all night last night thinking about that. I don't know who I am anymore. Does that make sense?"

"You've been through a lot."

"I have, and it isn't over yet. There's still the hearing."

"Have you heard from Hammer about it?"

"Not yet."

"I can follow up with him."

I looked off in the distance. "I can too, Edge."

"Right. Yes. You can."

"I need to figure out my life, and in order to do that, I need to be alone."

"I see."

"And I meant what I said. I will pay you back."

"There's nothing to pay back."

"You let me stay in your house."

"You were a guest. I don't charge my guests overnight accommodation fees."

"Okay, then, what about the clothes and other things you bought for me?"

"I believe I got more pleasure from your clothes than you did. The knickers in particular."

"You fixed my car."

"I'll concede that one. You may reimburse me for one battery."

"I don't want to think about what it cost for you to find Possum's killer…and all the other stuff I know nothing about."

"It was an investigation into a murder as well as into a domestic terrorist group. We'll be duly compensated."

"I have a hard time believing that Hays County is going to pay a group of private security people to solve their crimes."

Edge didn't respond, and I knew no matter how hard I pushed on this subject, he wouldn't.

"I'm staying with Tee-Tee."

"I know."

"It's only been two nights, but I think staying with her will have a positive impact on my life."

"I'm very glad to hear it."

"She apologized for what happened all those years ago. It ended up being a trick to get me to agree to live with her." I shook my head. "No, that isn't right. The apology part wasn't a trick."

"Rebel—"

"I think I know what you're about to say, Edge, but even if I'm wrong, I need you to understand that I'm unwilling to budge on this. There's never been a time in my life when I had the means to think about a future. I have that now. Thanks to you and Tee-Tee."

"Can I still see you?"

I smiled. "Define seeing me."

"Spend time with you like this. Go for rides. Talk."

"No sex, Edge. No baths, no trying to take care of me, no long, hard, deep kisses."

"Got it."

"That was too easy."

"There's nothing easy about it, Rebel. I can't accept you no longer being a part of my life. If it means I can't ever kiss you again in order to spend time with you, that's something I'll learn to accept."

When he turned his horse around, I followed him back to the barn. Had I really just told him no kissing? I must be out of my mind. On the other hand, for the first time ever, just like I'd told him, I was focusing on me. Me and no one else.

We'd dismounted and were cooling down the horses when Edge's cell phone rang. He pulled it out and looked at the screen. "It's Hammer. Shall I tell him to ring you directly?"

"It's okay, Edge. You can talk to him."

He ended the call a couple of minutes later, saying the hearing for the dismissal of the murder charge was scheduled for four this afternoon.

"I'll need to talk to Tee-Tee."

Edge nodded. "You go. I'll take care of your horse."

"Thanks." I handed him the reins and walked away.

"Hey, Rebel?" he shouted after me. "Good luck this afternoon."

I waved and kept walking as I let the weight of his words fall on my shoulders, and that's exactly what they did. Every step became drudgery as I realized I truly was on my own—just like I'd told him I wanted to be.

"I don't understand, *Mija*. I'm sure Edge would go with you if you asked."

"That's the point, *Tía*. I told him I wanted to do things on my own. He said he'd respect that. I can't turn right around and ask him to hold my hand."

"If I had more notice, I could go with you."

I smiled. "I appreciate that so much, but like I told Edge, I need to be independent. I need to figure out my life and what I want it to be on my own. The first step is this hearing. Once it's over, I'll be free."

I knew Tee-Tee didn't understand, and that had to be okay for both of us. I climbed into Susan and drove off the ranch, hoping that when I came back later, I'd be able to figure out how to get back in the gate.

"Where's Edge? Parking the truck?" Hammer asked when I approached him outside the courtroom.

"He didn't come."

"What? Why not?"

"It's my hearing."

"He's your custodian." Hammer rubbed his hand over his bald head and then pulled out his cell phone and walked away.

"Hey," a familiar voice said from behind me. "What's wrong with Hammer?"

I spun around and looked into Edge's eyes. "I just told him you wouldn't be here."

"I have to be. I'm your custodian."

"Why didn't you tell me that earlier?"

When Edge put his hands in his pockets, something told me he did it so he wasn't tempted to touch me.

"There you are!" shouted Hammer. "She said you weren't coming."

"Misunderstanding," Edge muttered and then winked at me.

"Let's get this over with."

Hammer motioned for Edge and me to go in front of him and then to the row where we should sit. As I turned to do so, someone in the back row caught my attention. My public defender was here. Obviously, he had other cases; however, there was no one else in the courtroom.

"What's wrong?" Edge whispered.

"The man in the back row. That's my former attorney."

Edge leaned over and told Hammer what I'd told him.

Hammer looked at both of us. "What the hell is John Lynch doing here?"

34

Edge

Rebel looked as sick as I felt. I thought back to the first day Hammer took over as her attorney and what he'd said. *"I don't understand why the judge didn't make the PD recuse himself. He's got a goddamn tie to the vic."*

His name was *Lynch.* Was it a coincidence? Given we weren't able to find anyone associated with the ABT with the same name, I had to believe it wasn't.

I looked into Rebel's wide eyes. "Let's get through the hearing."

"Okay," she mouthed.

I knew I shouldn't do it, but I couldn't help myself. I reached over and took her left hand in my right. Instead of pulling away, she covered both with her other hand. I felt mine begin to shake, but again, instead of pulling away, she held it tighter, and the shaking stopped.

If only I could go back and unsay all the ridiculous things I'd said to her. But would it change anything?

Wouldn't Rebel still want her independence? Still want to figure out the rest of her life on her own?

Her hands remained with mine, and that had to mean something. As she forged ahead in her new life alone, having me nearby, close even, might not be such a bad thing.

The dismissal of the charges against Rebel was a formality hurried along when Mac stopped in to ensure the judge knew the details of the case. He also explained he wouldn't be pressing charges for the death of the ranch hand. After his investigation, he told the judge he'd determined she acted in self-defense.

No mention was made of Rebel almost killing a federal agent. That part didn't surprise me. My assumption was that Rile had somehow smoothed that over with the feds.

Sometime in the midst of his appearance, I noticed Lynch leaving the courtroom. He'd be getting the full Invincible-style workup when I got back to the ranch later. If he had as much as a failing grade in secondary school, we'd know it.

"Do you have to get back right away?" I asked Rebel after we exited the courtroom and Hammer left.

"I guess not."

"What do you say we drive into Austin and celebrate?"

"Are you sure?"

"I'm not exactly certain what you're asking, but if it means I get to spend time with you, then, yes, I'm sure."

I had a favorite place on South Congress that I thought Rebel might enjoy, so I rang them while we were on our way to the truck and made a reservation. Then I had another idea.

"The Trail of Lights Festival along the river opened last weekend. We could walk through it and then have dinner a bit later."

"I've never been to Austin, so whatever you suggest sounds fine to me."

As Rebel and I walked through the myriad of Christmas light displays, it was painfully hard not to take her in my arms and kiss her. As difficult as it was, I vowed to respect her wishes and prayed that one day I could hold her once again.

"It's so beautiful," Rebel murmured when we walked through a tunnel of a million multicolored lights. "It's been so long since I've celebrated Christmas, I forgot how magical it can be."

My heart hurt thinking about her Christmases past and mine. I didn't remember many when I wasn't on a mission somewhere in the world where the holiday wasn't celebrated. Or if it was, I didn't partake.

"What would you say…no, never mind."

"No, tell me. What were you going to say?"

"It'll sound daft."

She smiled and tucked her arm in mine. "Tell me anyway."

"I was thinking of putting up a tree this year. I've no ornaments or other Christmas decorations, so… daft, right?"

"Ornaments don't necessarily make the tree, you know?"

"No?"

"There are so many other things we could do. String popcorn and cranberries. We could dry orange slices and hang them from ribbons, and tie cinnamon sticks together and do the same. Oh, and I've even seen oranges dotted with cloves." She tapped her finger to her bottom lip, something I'd noticed Tee-Tee often did. "One year, I remember my grandmother and I made ornaments. I think the recipe was half applesauce and half cinnamon. We rolled them out, used cookie cutters to make shapes, and then let them dry. They smelled so good."

"Sounds brilliant." Was she saying she wanted to do all these things with me? It sounded as though she was. "So…you wouldn't mind hanging out with me like that?"

"Like that?"

"You know. As friends."

"I'd love it."

After we'd made our way through the light show, we took a car service to South Congress. It was easier to leave the truck parked where it was than try to find a spot in the popular neighborhood where five-star restaurants dotted every block.

"Do you fancy Italian?" I asked as the driver wound his way through the crowded streets.

Rebel looked over at me and smiled. "I fancy English more." She had the sweetest look on her face.

Gawd, I wanted to kiss her.

"Hey, what are you two doin' here?" I heard a voice I didn't recognize say as we walked into the restaurant where I'd made the reservation. I turned in time to see Rebel wrap her arms around the Long Branch's former bouncer.

"Steel! It's so good to see you!" She pulled me closer. "You remember Edge?"

It must have dawned on her when he would've seen me last. Rather than a sweet smile, she frowned. I leaned forward and whispered in her ear. "None of that, now. We're celebrating new beginnings. That was in all of our pasts."

"Right," she said, a smile plastered back on her face. "So, Steel, is this where you work?"

He told us it was and then introduced us to some of the other staff. It seemed like a friendly bunch, and the clientele was nothing like those who frequented the Long Branch. Not that there was anything wrong with that group; this was just slightly higher brow.

After we finished a fabulous meal, during which we both ate far too much, the server Steel had insisted wait on us, brought a dessert tray to the table.

"Wow," Rebel said, her voice full of awe. "These are so beautiful. Do you make them in-house?"

At that very moment, Steel stopped back by. While Rebel continued to ooh and aah over the desserts, I filled him in on her job at the dining hall.

"You should taste the things she makes," I told him proudly.

"Hey, Rebel, you wanna meet the pastry chef?"

Her head spun so quickly I laughed.

"Seriously?"

Steel nodded. "I'll take you back to meet her."

"Would you mind?"

"Not in the least, sweetness."

She leaned over and kissed my cheek. "I'll be right back."

A few minutes later, Steel rejoined me. "They're still talking. I thought I'd keep you company."

"Appreciate that."

"You wanna tell me what went down?"

"How long will she be?"

"Long enough for the short version."

Steel was shaking his head when Rebel came back to the table.

"What did I miss?" she asked.

"Not a thing, dollface," he answered. "We missed you, though."

She rolled her eyes and punched his arm. "You were always such a flirt."

As I watched and listened to them banter, I realized that the Rebel seated beside me tonight, was likely the woman she'd been when her mother was still alive. Before the overdose, before Possum, before vengeance poisoned her beautiful soul. She smiled easily and laughed with her whole body. I'd seen so little of her this way. She was right when she said I didn't know her.

Rebel nudged me. "Why so glum?"

I shook my head. "Not glum at all. Just so bloody happy to see you smile."

She leaned in closer to me so only I could hear her. "You really do care about me, don't you, Edge?"

"More than you'll ever know."

"I hope that isn't true."

"What do you mean?"

"I want to know that you care about me."

"I do, sweetness."

"I have something to tell you."

I laughed. "You look like the cat who ate the canary."

She leaned closer still and whispered, "The pastry chef wants me to come back for an interview. To be her apprentice." Her face lit up like the thousands of Christmas lights we'd seen.

"That's fantastic!"

"You think so? I mean, what about Tee-Tee?"

"Discuss it with her. You should have no doubt that she'll be honest with you."

Rebel laughed out loud. "You have her pegged."

Thoughts raced through my mind. Would she have to move away from the ranch? Live in Austin full-time? And more worrying, was there a connection between her former attorney and the threat the now-dead ranch hand had delivered?

"This is like a dream come true," I heard her say under her breath after Steel left us alone. "And all because you brought me to Austin."

"I'd say fate put you here more than I."

Rebel shook her head. "No, Edge. Every good thing that has happened to me in the last couple of weeks has been because of you."

"I appreciate that, sweetness, but you're giving me too much credit."

She turned her body so she faced me. "There's something else I need to tell you."

35

Rebel

The look on Edge's face broke my heart. The man had done so much for me, and he'd come to expect that whatever I said would be something bad.

Like he'd done to me so many times, I cupped his cheek with my palm. "I don't want you to say anything, okay?"

He nodded and I smiled. "Good boy."

Edge shook his head and laughed.

"I told you before that both Tee-Tee and Casper warned me not to mess things up with you, and I told you my fear that I would, because that's what I do."

He kept his eyes glued to mine but didn't speak.

"After Casper stopped by the dining hall to apologize, as she was leaving, I told her I owed her my life. She said I was wrong, that I owed my life to you. Don't," I added when he tried to shake his head. "It's true, Edge. The night you pulled Possum off me in the parking lot, you saved my life."

That he seemed to accept.

"And then you continued. Maybe you didn't save my life in the same dramatic way you did that night, but you gave me a life. I made one meal, and you immediately picked up on my dream to be a chef. No one knew that. Not even my mother. Yet, you knew it right away. It was your idea to ask Tee-Tee if I could work in the dining hall. I really don't know how to thank you."

His eyes darted back and forth between mine.

"You can talk now."

"I know exactly how you can thank me, Rebel."

"Bake you an orange cake?"

He smiled. "Be happy. Embrace your life and live it to the fullest. Nothing will bring me more joy."

"Again, nothing for yourself, only for me."

"Believe me, I'm not as selfless as you may think. It's taken every ounce of self-control I possess not to touch you, kiss you, pull you into my arms, and never let go. But I care so much for you, I will do anything to respect your wishes. Even if that means letting you go."

The idea that he would, made my heart hurt, but it's what I'd asked of him. "I still want us to be friends, Edge."

"We are, sweetness."

"We'll decorate your Christmas tree together, right?"

"I won't do it without you."

After taking a car service to Edge's truck, our drive back to his house was quiet. I had no idea what he was thinking about. Maybe it was the possibility I'd be leaving the ranch. Or maybe it was the public defender showing up in court today.

"I never put it together."

"What's that, sweetness?"

"My lawyer and Lynch. I only met with him a couple of times, but you'd think I would've remembered his name."

"Even if you had, our approach would've remained as it was."

"Do you think I'm in danger, Edge?"

He scrubbed his face with his hand.

"You aren't answering."

"Right. My answer for now is that I'm not certain. I intend to do some investigating on my own to determine whether or not I believe Mr. Lynch poses a threat."

"Do you really think I should tell Tee-Tee about the apprenticeship?"

He looked at me and smiled. "You know the answer."

"You think I should?"

"For now, it's an interview. I've no doubt you'll be offered the position, but address that with her once you have."

"Susan is at the courthouse."

He smiled again. "I remember. I was thinking you might want to pick *her* up tomorrow."

"Thank you for not making fun of me over naming my car, and yes, tomorrow would be easier. I'm sure Tee-Tee can give me a ride."

"I'll take you to get Susan."

"Edge…"

He reached over and took my hand. "Until we're certain that there's no connection between the threat against you and your former public defender, please let me continue to ensure your safety."

"Thank you," I murmured as his thumb continued to stroke the back of my hand.

It was midafternoon before I had a chance to take a break. One of the other cooks had taken a sick day, so Tee-Tee and I were busier than normal. The interview I'd yet to schedule was on my mind constantly.

Every time I tried to bring it up, either she or I were interrupted.

"*Mija,* where is your mind?" she asked when I went into the storeroom and came back without the one thing she'd asked me to fetch.

"I'm sorry, *Tía.*"

"Come and sit. Tell me what happened yesterday."

"We don't have time, dinner is—"

She sighed and folded her arms. "The way things are going with you, dinner won't be ready until tomorrow anyway. Now, *¡siéntate!*"

I pulled a chair up next to her desk and told her everything from my attorney thinking Edge wasn't coming, to seeing my public defender, and finally, to seeing Steel at the restaurant in Austin. The one thing I didn't tell her about was the conversation I'd had with their pastry chef.

She rested her hand on mine. "Something is troubling you. I can feel it. Is it the lawyer?"

I shrugged. "Partially. And Edge. He's so good to me, *Tía.* I feel like such a bitch for leaving in the first place, but now that I have, I know it's the right thing for me. I can't just live with him, because the sex is off the charts. Ya know?"

As soon as I said the words, I realized what words I'd said. "I'm sorry, *Tía.* That was inappropriate."

She sat back in her chair. "Do you think I don't have sex?"

"Uh…no…I…um…"

"I…um," she mimicked. "You aren't the only one who had a hot date last night."

I raised my eyebrows.

"That's right, *Mija.* "

I hoped she didn't continue. I knew the point she was trying to make without needing her to go into graphic detail.

"What do you want, *Mija*?"

I had no idea. I'd gone from having zero choices in my life to having too many. I took a deep breath, knowing that if I put it off any longer, I'd only continue stressing myself out. I closed both my eyes and blurted, "The pastry chef at the restaurant Edge took me to in Austin asked me to come back for an interview to be her apprentice."

I slowly opened one eye and then the other, so afraid of the look I'd see on Tee-Tee's face. There were tears in her eyes, but she didn't look unhappy. She took both my hands in hers and squeezed. "Oh, Lucy! I'm so happy for you!"

"It's just an interview, *Tía*."

"Tell me more about it. What did she say? Don't leave anything out. I want to know every word."

I'd just finished reiterating the conversation to her, repeating certain things two and three times, when we heard someone enter through the dining hall's front door. It was far too early for anyone to be here for dinner.

I stood slowly and put my hand on the gun tucked into my waistband.

36

Edge

There was no easy way to tell Rebel that her car was gone. It wasn't actually *gone,* but the extent of the damage done by the vandalism made it impossible to repair. The harder part was telling her it wasn't a random act. The messages spray-painted on the exterior were directed at her personally.

"What's wrong?" she asked, approaching me slowly.

"I have unfortunate news."

"Should I sit down?"

"It might be a good idea."

I sat too, and she reached for my hand. "Just tell me, Edge." I remembered the times I said those same words to her.

"Susan was broken into last night. There was extensive damage. Irreparable, in fact."

Rebel leaned back and put her hand on her heart. "Oh my God. You scared me. I was sure you were going to tell me someone died."

Her eyes bored into mine when I showed no sign of relief at her reaction.

"There's more, isn't there?"

"I'm afraid there is. Whoever did it, intended to send a clear message."

"It isn't over, is it?"

I slowly shook my head.

"What do I do?"

"For now, there's nothing for you to do. Continue on as you are. As long as you're on the ranch, you're safe."

"I wasn't before."

"Right. And believe me, additional measures have been implemented to ensure that you are."

"Do I have to come back to live with you?"

I put my hand on my heart, hoping for a moment of levity. "I will spare you such torture, sweetness."

As I hoped she would, Rebel smiled.

"We'll find who did this, just like we found Possum's killer. I promise you."

"I guess the interview is a no-go, then."

I'd given that a lot of thought on my way back from the courthouse after Mac had called to ask me to come and see the vandalism for myself. I hated the idea that this lovely woman would be forced to put a dream on hold due to the likes of criminals. It was a tragedy, really.

"No. Schedule your interview."

"But—"

"If not by me, you'll be escorted to and from by a member of our team. And that is in the event we haven't yet located those still posing a threat to you."

"Okay."

I motioned with my head toward the kitchen. "Have you spoken with Tee-Tee?"

"Yes, and she's very excited about it."

"It's because she loves you."

"You're making this very hard on me."

"I'm sorry."

"Aren't you going to ask what I meant?"

"Very well. What did you mean?"

"Keeping things between us as just friends."

I closed my eyes and smiled. "I'm not sure how to respond."

Rebel stood, put her hands on my shoulders, leaned forward, and kissed my cheek. "Thank you, Edge."

After agreeing to come back to the dining hall for dinner, I called a meeting. Rile had returned to London, but Grinder was still here as were Decker and I. On my way to my place, I rang Mac as well as Hammer. If Rebel's former attorney was somehow involved, Hammer's assistance could be helpful.

One by one, they arrived at the house. Grinder, whom I'd expected to show up first, was last. The moment he walked in, I knew something was off.

"What is it?" I asked before he walked over to join the others.

He looked up at me as if he was surprised by my question. "Nothing."

I raised a brow.

"Unrelated."

"Anything we should discuss?"

"Not now."

I accepted his responses in the way I always did. Grinder would talk when he was ready, and no amount of pushing would ever change that. Oddly, the same was not true when it came to me. The man could be relentless. I suppose that's what made us best mates. He knew that, ultimately, I needed to talk things out. Conversely, I knew he didn't. At least not until he was ready.

"Thanks for agreeing to meet so expediently," I began as I tossed the photos I'd taken of Rebel's car onto the table. It was almost unrecognizable, given the amount of damage done.

"Any security footage?" Decker asked.

Mac shook his head. "Only of them knocking out the cameras."

"They knew where they all were."

"Hays County doesn't have the resources you have here at the ranch. They aren't very well hidden. In fact, we use them as a deterrent, more than surveillance."

Among the symbols of hate painted over the majority of the exterior was the same threat issued to Rebel by the ranch hand. Essentially, that she'd pay for Possum's death, one way or another.

"It seems our circumventing the coup at the Aryan Brotherhood of Texas was more of a byproduct of our infiltration rather than neutralizing the threat against Rebel."

The men at the table nodded their agreement.

"Hammer, how much do you know about John Lynch?"

"Boring little fucker. Been practicing law longer than I have and is still a PD. What does that tell ya?"

"Decker?"

"There's nothing, Edge. When Hammer says Lynch is boring, it's an appropriate description. He's got no links to the ABT, and his link to Possum was a big enough stretch that I understand why the judge didn't ask for his recusal."

"Hammer, you seemed to believe otherwise."

"I have a different moral code than many of my fellow attorneys. Any connection to the opposition is grounds for recusing a case."

"What was the connection?" asked Mac.

"Second cousin, thrice removed."

"For Christ's sake, does anyone understand that shit? They were cousins. Isn't that enough?"

"As a point of law—" Decker began.

"Fuck the point of law," muttered Mac. "They had a connection. I'm with Hammer. He should've recused himself. That he didn't, makes him suspicious in my book."

"Logical too that he'd know where the courthouse cameras were located," said Hammer.

"A three-year-old would know where the cameras were," mumbled Grinder, the first words he'd said since we were seated.

"Are we in agreement that whoever is posing this threat is operating outside of the ABT?" I asked.

"For now," answered Decker. "We'll keep an open mind, however."

"No need to send anyone else in, then?" I confirmed.

"Agreed."

"Mac, are you working your sources?"

"Damn straight."

"I'm checking footage from area businesses. Maybe the vandals missed a feed somewhere," said Decker.

I filled them in on the possibility that Rebel would be traveling to and from Austin, and potentially working there.

"That complicates things. What's your intention?" asked Decker.

"Fixed around-the-clock surveillance."

"Has she moved back in?" asked Grinder.

I shook my head. "No, but I've got it covered."

"I'll be your second."

I would've asked, eventually, but given his current mood, his offer surprised me.

As the other three men were leaving, I asked him to stick around.

"Fancy a pint?"

"Sure."

I handed him a beer and a glass and joined him at the breakfast bar. "Not going to England for the holidays, then?"

Grinder leaned forward and put his head in his hands.

"Talk to me, mate."

"No. I'm not."

"Right."

I sat back in the stool and looked out the windows at the rolling hills of King-Alexander Ranch. I often thought I could happily spend the rest of my days right where I was. Would that be enough for me? I worried that it wouldn't. The idea that someone, namely Rebel, would be by my side made it seem more sustainable.

If she were to follow her dreams, she wouldn't be here, though. She'd be in Austin. To me, any city was just that. They all blended into one another at some point.

The question begged, why was I putting so much stock in the possibility of a relationship with her? I'd told her that the amount of time we spent together was irrelevant, but was my sudden desire to settle down circumventing all logic? Was it more about me than her?

I didn't believe it was, but it was certainly a thought worthy of consideration.

I found myself wanting to talk to my brother again. There were times in our lives when I could've gone weeks, perhaps even months, without doing so, but in this, I needed his counsel.

"I'm getting a Christmas tree. Rebel and I are going to decorate it with popcorn," I blurted.

"You're off your trolley."

"Maybe not, Grind. Maybe for the first time in my life, I want to make memories rather than just avoid looking back."

The sadness I saw in my friend's eyes cut me to my core. So many times in the years I'd known him, I wished I could do something—anything—to help him. Like now, I felt powerless to make a difference.

"I'm not ready to talk about it."

I walked over to the fridge and pulled out two more bottles of beer, steeling myself against any reaction whatsoever. Never before had I heard those words. I was stunned.

"Get over yourself," he said, yanking one of the bottles from my hand. "I'm not suggesting we start a quilting circle."

"A quilting circle?"

"You know what I mean, ya wanker."

"I love her."

Grinder nodded. "We all know that, Edge."

"Why doesn't she?"

"Gonna take something a lot stronger than a pint to answer that one."

37

Rebel

I promised Tee-Tee I wouldn't be gone long on the day of my interview, even though she said it wasn't necessary for me to hurry back. However, I couldn't see myself feeling good about interviewing for one job while shirking the responsibilities of another.

The pastry chef, Susan—which, yes, I found ironic—told me late mornings were best for her to meet. After breakfast was served and the kitchen was clean at the dining hall, Edge drove me to Austin.

"I appreciate this."

"Yes."

"Edge…are you listening to me?"

"Of course."

He seemed distracted, but then, so was I. I was far too nervous to focus on a conversation, so I don't know why I was trying to start one.

I looked out the window and took several deep breaths. There was a part of me that had already decided Susan was granting me the interview solely as a favor to Steel. A much smaller part of me hoped that I, at least, had a chance at the apprenticeship.

When we spoke on the phone to schedule the appointment, Susan told me it wasn't a full-time position. I'd be required to be at the restaurant three days a week—Thursday, Friday, and Saturday. At some point, I would also work Friday and Saturday evenings to help plate dessert when the restaurant was busy.

"Who will you say you are?" I asked Edge, suddenly realizing how unprofessional it would look if I brought a man with me. Would they think he was my boyfriend? It would probably make it worse if I told them he was more of a bodyguard.

"I've worked it out with Steel."

I didn't know what that meant, but I guess I didn't need to.

Lingering in the back of my mind was what I would do for transportation if I was actually offered the position. It wasn't like I'd made enough money to save for another car.

When Edge pulled up a few doors down from the restaurant, I saw Steel waiting nearby.

"Break a wooden spoon," he said as I got out of the car.

"Thanks. I'm nervous."

"You'll do great."

I could see the sincerity in his eyes. No one had ever been as good to me as Edge was. I wouldn't have dared to dream that one day I'd have a boyfriend that was anything like him—not that that's what he was. We were friends, at least I hoped we could be.

"Susan has everything ready," Steel told me as he unlocked the door and escorted me into the closed restaurant.

The interview went far differently than I'd anticipated. It was more of an introductory meeting and tour. When I explained I had no formal training nor had I attended school for a job like this one, her only response was, "Good. I won't have to break your bad habits."

I filled out the employee paperwork, gave her my sizes for my uniform, and we agreed on a start date after the first of the year. As she'd told me on the phone, I was expected to be at the restaurant Thursday through Saturday mornings, and would add Friday and Saturday evenings after the first two-week trial period.

By the time Steel walked me out, my mind was reeling.

"I got the apprenticeship," I told him once we were outside where Edge was waiting.

"I knew you did."

"How? I mean, she barely interviewed me."

"You'll have to ask Tee-Tee." Sometimes I forgot how small Barton Creek was. Of course Steel would know Tee-Tee.

I looked at Edge, who shrugged and then congratulated me.

"See you in January," said Steel, hugging me. "And have a Merry Christmas."

"Right. Thanks. You too."

Edge opened the door of the car, and I stopped before I got in. The urge to kiss him was so overwhelming. I couldn't, though.

"Whose car is this?" I asked when he came around and got in the driver's side. I'd been so preoccupied on the drive here, I hadn't noticed it.

"Mine," he answered nonchalantly.

"It's gorgeous." I ran my hands over the buttery leather, completely overwhelmed by the dashboard that looked like it belonged in an airplane.

"I was wondering…"

I waited, but Edge didn't finish his sentence.

"What?"

"Did you still want to help me decorate a tree?"

To be honest, I'd forgotten all about it, but not because I didn't want to.

"I'd love to, but, Edge, are you sure you do?"

"I wouldn't have mentioned it if I didn't."

Those were the last words he said until we were through the ranch gates.

"Well?" asked Tee-Tee the minute I walked in.

"I got it."

"Don't sound so excited."

"I am excited. According to Steel, you had something to do with it. Thank you."

"*Mija*, what's going on?"

I slunk down in the chair. There was no point in lying. "Something's up with Edge."

"What do you mean?"

"The best way I can describe it is, you know how I am right now? That's how he was the whole way back."

"Maybe he has a lot on his mind."

"He asked me to help him decorate a Christmas tree."

Tee-Tee's eyebrows shot up.

"My reaction too."

"Come and sit."

Since whenever I ignored that request, she yelled at me, I went along willingly.

"It's possible to find yourself without pushing everyone out of your life, *Mija.*"

"I'm not pushing him out of my life; I'm taking a step back. We're still friends."

"With rules."

"What's your point?"

"Why not let things happen naturally? Instead of feeling like you have to be romantic, or can't be romantic, just be. If you want to kiss him, just do it. If you don't, well, then you're *estúpida.* My point is, how can either of you feel comfortable when you're together if you're so worried about what you can and can't do, can and can't say?"

"I already told him I only wanted to be friends."

"You changed your mind. If you want, you can always tell him that you're *estúpida.*"

"That I am or that you said I am?"

Tee-Tee patted my hand. "Both, *Mija.* Now, what's for dessert tonight?"

I'd decided earlier to make peppermint brownies. They were easy, and with the addition of mint, they'd be Christmas-y too. I dug out my cell phone—Edge's cell phone that I still needed to return to him—and sent him a text.

I've been thinking about the Christmas tree.

Moments later, he responded. *Change your mind?*

I had changed my mind, but not about the tree. *I think we should go and get one tonight.*

While he hadn't responded to my text, I was happy to see him in the dining hall for dinner. Grinder was with him, which I didn't recall happening before. The man laughed and smiled often enough, especially when he was around Edge, but it always seemed as though he had an underlying sadness. Maybe that's why they were best friends. After losing his parents at such a young age, Edge probably carried sadness too. Just like I did because of my mother's addiction.

Once I had the brownies plated with a dollop of fresh whipped cream, I grabbed a tray and took three portions to their table.

"Hi, guys." When I set the tray on the table, Edge got up and pulled out the chair next to him.

I gave him what I hoped was my sweetest smile. "Thank you."

"By all means." He sat back down, seemingly leaving my smile unnoticed.

I set one plate in front of him, one in front of Grinder, and took one for myself.

"This looks fantastic." Grinder looked at Edge as though he expected his friend to say something, but he didn't, nor did he take a bite of the brownie.

"Don't you like chocolate?"

"Sorry, what?"

"I asked if you liked chocolate."

He looked at the plate and then up at me. "Not terribly hungry."

My eye caught the brief look of surprise on Grinder's face.

"Okay, well, I'll leave you gentlemen to finish your conversation." I didn't wait for Edge to respond; I stood and walked away.

"Rebel, wait." Edge jumped up and followed me.

I stopped and took a deep breath before I turned around. "I'm sorry I interrupted."

He looked down at the floor. "You didn't."

"Is it me, Edge, or is something else going on?"

He looked up and into my eyes. "I'm truly happy that you were offered the position."

"I can tell." I half laughed, remembering how Tee-Tee had said the same words to me this afternoon.

He looked over his shoulder and then led me out the dining hall entryway. "I think we should forgo the tree decorating."

"Tonight or at all?"

"At all."

I bit my bottom lip, trying my hardest not to cry. I wasn't a six-year-old; I was a grown woman. I shouldn't be crying over a Christmas tree.

"I'm not sure I can do this."

"This?"

"You. Me. Friends. I know it makes me a wanker. Maybe after some time passes, but…"

"Say it, Edge."

He shook his head. "I sound like a sprog."

I cocked my head.

"Loose translation: baby."

I laughed. "I'm fighting tears over the disappointment of not getting a Christmas tree. Who's the sprog?"

He laughed too, and I loved the sound of it.

"I'm not sure I can do it either. You know…you, me, friends."

The smile left his face, and he nodded. "I understand. Completely."

"I mean, what's it been? Two days? I'm already failing miserably."

This time, he cocked his head.

I waved my hand in the direction of the dining hall. "If not for the room full of ranch hands, I'd kiss you… long and deep and hard."

"Bugger me," he muttered and then picked me up like he had so many times before and carried me out the front door. He set me on my feet, grasped the back of my neck, and brought his lips to mine.

His kiss was soft at first and then probing. He moved his hand from my neck to the back of my head and held me in place as he devoured my mouth. He kissed me so hard it hurt, but I wanted more.

Edge backed me up against the building and lifted me so his hands were on my bottom and my legs were around his waist. He rested his forehead against mine, and I could feel his hardness grow as he pressed against me.

"It has been so bloody hard to keep my hands off you." His fingers dug into my ass cheeks. "I can't be with you and not touch you, Rebel. I know that makes me weak, but I can't do it."

"I can't do it either." I kissed him again, pushing him like he'd done to me. "Take me home, Edge."

38

Edge

I couldn't get Rebel there quickly enough. Grinder had ridden to the hall with me, but when he came out and saw my car gone, he'd figure out what happened.

I held the passenger door open, and before she got in, Rebel leaned forward and thrust her tongue in my mouth. At the same time, she grabbed the crotch of my trousers.

"Earlier, when we were in Austin, this is what I wanted to do. I came so close." She massaged my cock with the palm of her hand. I pulled away, and she eased herself onto the seat.

"When I get in, I want to see your tits, Rebel." I closed the door and stalked around to the driver's side. I got in and started the car without taking my eyes off her as she unfastened the buttons on her blouse. "Speed it up."

If she didn't, I might've ripped it open. As she reached around to unfasten her bra, I pulled the cups down. I wanted those nipples in my mouth so badly I could taste them. I threw the car into reverse and sped off in the direction of my house.

"Play with them. Let me see you pinch them."

I didn't have to ask twice. Rebel groaned, and her head fell back when she pinched her nipples with her fingertips.

"Harder." I reached over with one hand and cupped her mound. "Are you wet for me, Rebel?"

"You know I am, Edge. I want you so much." She took one hand from her tit and put it over mine. "Harder, Edge."

I pulled into the garage and cut the engine. "I want you to go inside. As you walk from the door into the bedroom, I want you to strip. Leave the clothes on the floor as you take them off and wait for me on the bed. Do you understand me?" I asked when she looked at me with wide eyes.

"Yes."

"Go, Rebel. Naked on the bed, with your legs spread."

"Yes, Edge." With hooded eyes, she got out of the car.

I counted to thirty and then followed, leaving pieces of my clothing on the floor along the way, like I'd told her to. When I reached the bedroom, naked as she was,

I rested my knees on the bench at the end of the bed and focused on her glistening pussy.

"Touch yourself, Rebel. Spread yourself open for me."

She cried out in pleasure, her whole body writhing for me. I walked to the edge of the bed and stroked my finger over her collarbone and along the curve of her neck. Her nipples were puckered, hard, and begging for my mouth.

"Do you want me, Rebel?"

"You know I do, Edge."

"Where?"

"Everywhere."

I'd told her once that if she wanted it, to ask. If she wanted me everywhere, that's what she'd get.

"Tell me, Rebel, can you behave or, shall I restrain you?"

She moved her head from side to side. "I don't know."

I bit the side of her breast, and she cried out.

"Where should your hands be, Rebel?" I asked when I noticed her pulling at the bedclothes.

"Here?" she asked, bringing them back to her pussy.

"If you keep your hands where they belong and your legs spread for me, I won't restrain you."

Her only response was to plead with her eyes.

"What do you want first? My mouth, my fingers, or my cock?"

"I want it all," she moaned.

"So greedy."

"I can't get enough of you, Edge."

"The first thing we need to do is make sure you're never tempted to tell me again that we're 'just friends.'"

Her eyes opened wide.

"I've been waiting for this for two long days. Tell me you'll never make me wait again, little Rebel."

"I won't. I promise."

"Good." I moved her hands. "Put those over your head." I stroked a finger from her clit to her opening, swirling through her wetness. "Such a pretty pussy, and all for me." I licked her clit repeatedly and slid one finger inside her.

"Edge, please."

"Now, for your punishment. I want you to watch me, sweetness."

She moaned again and arched against my mouth.

I tortured her with my mouth and fingers until the only thing she could do was beg. "Please, God. Please fuck me, Edge. I can't stand it."

"I think you've learned your lesson."

"I have. I promise."

I smiled and kissed her, thrusting my tongue into her mouth. The whimpers I felt vibrating from her mouth into mine, were the sweetest sound I'd ever heard. Like her, I couldn't stand it any longer. I grabbed a condom from the drawer.

Once sheathed, I entered her with one powerful thrust, pushing through her convulsing pussy. She began to thrash under me, her wet warmth pulling me in deeper.

Rebel whimpered and cried, begging for a release. When I brought my fingers to her clit and pinched, her scream tore through the room. Once I gave her the first orgasm, I pulled back, torturing her all over again, until finally, my cock swelled and I gave in to the incredible feeling of releasing the days of frustration into her body.

"No Christmas tree tonight," she murmured before her breathing evened out.

Exhausted, every bit of pleasure wrung out of both of us, we slept.

I woke her two more times before the alarm went off. When it did, we both rolled from the bed and let the warm water from the double-headed shower soothe our aching muscles.

I felt a calmness emanating from Rebel, which mirrored my own sense of peace. The angst of having to keep my hands off her dissipated, and in its place, I felt whole, complete, no longer questioning, just accepting. For now, we didn't need to define what we were to each other. I hoped I wasn't wrong in believing Rebel felt the same way I did.

We spent the next week in each other's arms as much as her work schedule at the dining hall would allow.

We put up a Christmas tree one night and took two more to decorate it, adding the homemade ornaments little by little until we both agreed our tree was full.

I'd avoided everything to do with the holiday for so long that I'd forgotten how genuinely happy it made me.

While Rebel worked, I delighted in finding gifts for her. I'd agreed to her request not to be extravagant, which made finding small things I knew she'd treasure, so much more satisfying.

I spoke with Lennox twice about the holiday, and after the second, we agreed we'd spend it apart but without regret, given how happy each of us felt.

We planned to celebrate Christmas Eve with Tee-Tee and Boon so we could spend the next day and night on our own.

"What about Grinder?" she'd asked the week before.

"I'll check, but my prediction is he'll decline any invitation we offer."

The morning of Christmas Eve, I dropped Rebel off at the dining hall and sent a text to Grinder, letting him know I would be stopping by. I hadn't seen him except in passing since the first night Rebel and I spent back together. Whenever I did, he expressed his happiness for us. Any attempt on my part to get him to talk went the way it always did, with Grinder shutting down and making an excuse for either him or me to leave. This morning was very different.

When he greeted me, it looked as though he hadn't slept in days. He had dark circles under his eyes, his hair was unkempt, and it appeared he'd lost weight in the two or three days since I last saw him.

"I've come to talk to you about Christmas," I said, eyeing the travel bag that sat just inside the front door. "Going somewhere?"

"Have a seat," he said, pointing to a chair at the kitchen table.

"I don't want to keep you."

"I'm leaving for a while, Edge. I don't know exactly how long I'll be gone."

"Are you okay?"

He nodded. "It's Pia."

The woman had been a part of Grinder's life since before we became friends while at the Military Academy in Sandhurst. They'd met on holiday when they were teenagers, before Grinder joined the Armed Forces of the Crown, before his time in Iraq.

I didn't know her well. In fact, I'd only met her a couple of times, and while Grinder had only talked of what happened between them once, I knew the way he felt about her ran deep.

"Is she okay?"

His response left me reeling.

39

Rebel

Something had been off with Edge since yesterday morning. Every attempt I made to find out what, was met with reassurances from him that everything was fine, and not to worry.

His stress sat so close to the surface, I couldn't help but see it. He flexed his right hand more often than usual, his jaw was clenched, and when he was deep in thought, his brow furrowed. It was almost time for us to leave for Tee-Tee's, and I couldn't stand it any longer.

I found him in the gym, sitting on the weight bench.

"If you don't want to go to Tee-Tee's, we don't have to. And if celebrating Christmas with me tomorrow is too much, just say so."

He slowly looked up, and his eyes met mine. "What's this, Rebel?"

"You've been so stressed. You say it's nothing, but it is, Edge. You asked me to tell you if there's something bothering me instead of pulling away. This is me telling you."

He stood, walked over to me, and cupped my cheek with his palm. "I'm sorry, Rebel. I promise it isn't you. It's nothing to do with us."

"Do you need to leave?"

His eyes scrunched momentarily, and then his face softened. "No, this isn't work either."

I took a step back so he was no longer touching me. "What is it, then? If you aren't going to tell me, then—"

"Stop. Please. I need you to trust me. Believe me when I tell you that while I do have something on my mind, it isn't anything to do with us." He scrubbed his face with his hand. "I cannot be specific, Rebel. I promised I wouldn't betray a confidence, but it's about Grinder."

I sat down on the weight bench, and Edge sat beside me. I felt such relief that it truly wasn't anything to do with me, but it was quickly replaced with worry for Edge's best friend. "Is there anything I can do?"

Edge smiled and shook his head. "You're sweet to ask. I wish there was something either of us could do, but there isn't."

"Did you invite him to spend Christmas Eve with us?"

"I did, but he has other plans."

"Christmas Day?"

"He left town. I'm not sure how long he'll be away."

"If anything changes, will you tell me?"

"I'll tell you as much as I can."

Christmas Eve dinner was a hodge-podge of ethnic dishes. Tee-Tee made tamales and Posole Rojo, and Boon grilled rib eye steaks. I was responsible for an appetizer or salad as well as dessert. I made *Ensalada de Noche Buena*—a traditional Mexican salad with lettuce, beets, fruit, and peanuts tossed in a light orange vinaigrette.

The dessert I chose was a surprise for Edge. I'd made the traditional English Christmas pudding seven days ago and hoped that it was long enough in advance for the flavors to mature. To my delight, he said it was the best he'd ever had.

By request, I made a pan of cinnamon rolls for us to have Christmas morning. It was afternoon by the time we ate any, and evening before we opened our gifts. Instead, we lay in bed most of the day, telling each other stories about the Christmases of our childhood. Maybe it was because I was with Edge instead of alone, but so many happy memories popped up for me—things I hadn't thought about in years.

While he didn't say so specifically, I guessed Edge felt the same way just by the smile on his face and the glint in his eyes when he told me stories about his parents and his brother.

When it turned dark, Edge built a fire and we sat in front of our tree full of things we'd made together, and gave each other gifts. I only had one for him. I hoped he'd like it.

"You first," he said, handing me a wrapped box.

"How many are there?" I asked, trying to look around him.

"You'll see. Now, open it."

There was a definite theme to the gifts he gave me. My favorite among the kitchen tools and utensils was a blank cookbook. "I want you to fill every page with all my favorites," he told me.

"It will take me years to fill this."

He leaned over and kissed me. "Precisely. I have one more for you."

"Let me give you yours first." I got up and went behind the tree to where I'd hidden his gift.

"It's so much more fun to watch you as you open yours," he said when I set the box on his lap.

"It isn't much," I murmured. "But it's sentimental."

"This is the best Christmas I've ever had." There was so much love in his eyes when he spoke, I almost cried.

"Me too."

Gingerly, he opened the lid and pulled out the watch that rested inside. "That belonged to my grandfather," I said while he examined it like the treasure it was.

"Are you sure about giving it to me?"

"Absolutely. I want you to have it, Edge."

"Time for yours." He reached behind him and pulled out a very small package the size of a ring box.

"Before you race from the room, terrified that I've gone too far, it isn't what you might think."

He handed it to me, and I opened the lid. Inside was a necklace that looked like it might be a family heirloom, like my grandfather's watch was.

"It's a locket," he said, pointing to the clasp.

I opened it, and inside were two photos I recognized. One was of him, cut out from the photo I first saw of him with his family. The other was of me, cut from the photo taken with my mother when I was seven years old.

"Don't worry, I made copies of the photos first. It belonged to my mum." He took it out of the box and fastened it around my neck.

"I love it so much."

"I promised you I wouldn't go too far, but, Rebel, I have to tell you what's in my heart."

I fingered the locket and looked into his eyes, unable to speak.

"I've never felt the way I feel about you before." He cupped my cheek with his palm. "I care for you in a way I never believed possible."

"I feel the same way about you, Edge."

"I never want to lose you, Lucy 'Rebel' Marks."

I leaned forward and kissed him, afraid that if I didn't, I'd say the three words I didn't think either of us was ready for.

40

Rebel

One month later

There had to be a better word for the level of exhaustion I felt. Whatever it was, would also have to be combined with elation.

My first two weeks at the restaurant were a dream come true. I loved working with Tee-Tee in the ranch's dining hall, but owning my own place someday had been one of those pie-in-the-sky fantasies I'd never admitted to anyone. Just working in one, even as an apprentice, felt as though I was one step closer.

Edge had rented a small house for us to stay in the four days a week we had to be in Austin. We'd arrive sometime on Wednesday and then drive back either late Saturday night or Sunday morning, and stay at the ranch until it was time to head back to the city. While he told me it was because he couldn't stand to be away from me, I knew without needing confirmation that the issue of who "Lynch" was, was still lingering in the back of both of our minds.

Christy, one of the waitresses, had been trying to get me to hang out after work all week, but at the end of my shift, I couldn't wait to get back to Edge and tell him about my day.

As I was leaving the night before, Christy stopped me on my way out. "Tomorrow's Friday, you know, payday? Please stay and have at least one drink with us."

"I'll see," I told her. "But not more than one." As the apprentice pastry chef, I had to be at the restaurant earlier than almost everyone else in order to have time to prep before my boss arrived. Being late was not an option. Neither was being hungover.

I didn't add that before I committed to staying later tomorrow, I wanted to talk it over with Edge. I hadn't told her, or anyone else, anything about him. The only person who knew he was here in Austin with me was Steel.

When I mentioned the invitation to Edge as we lay in bed, he encouraged me to accept. "Part of any job is the camaraderie with your fellow employees."

"Do you want to join us?"

"Maybe next time. Have fun and get to know them on your own."

He never said what he did all day and night while I was at work, and I didn't ask.

"There you are, Lucy," Christy said to me the next night. "I thought maybe you'd sneaked out the back." She motioned for me to take the barstool next to her.

I noticed a few employees weren't seated. "I can stand."

"Don't be silly. We've been holding this open for you."

"Why?"

Christy laughed. "I told you how she was. Lucy, you're on your feet more than the rest of us, and you start earlier too. I don't know how you do it, girl."

Apart from my crappy waitressing job at the Barton Creek Diner, where I'd never considered "hanging out" with a soul who worked there, I hadn't been around industry people. It never occurred to me it might be fun until Edge mentioned "camaraderie." That's exactly how I felt, sitting and listening to them all talk about their shifts.

The restaurant where we worked was busy all the time, which meant the waitstaff made great tips, plus the kitchen staff was well paid. It was nice to be around so many happy people. It was inexplicable, then, when a few minutes later, a feeling of foreboding settled over me. I tried my best to ignore it, and even thought about calling Edge. When I looked over my shoulder and Steel winked at me from his perch near the front door, I felt a little better.

Not ten minutes later, the bartender, Barney, walked over and motioned for me to come closer. "There are a couple guys over there who said to buy Rebel a drink, and when I told them I didn't know who that was, they pointed at you."

I didn't want to turn around and look to see who was there, but curiosity was killing me.

Barney wagged his finger at me again. "Look in the mirror over there. They can't see you, but you can see them."

The restaurant was dimly lit, so I couldn't get a good look at their faces.

"Know who they are?" Barney asked.

"I'm not sure."

He lowered his hand and made a circular motion with his index finger.

"What's going on?" I asked Christy when the staff with us at the bar moved in closer.

"It's what we do when one of us is getting unwanted attention," she whispered.

"I don't want to cause any problems."

She rolled her eyes. "It happens all the time. Those cowboy types don't like taking no for an answer. Don't get me wrong, my daddy's a cowboy, but not the same as the likes of them. You can kinda tell, ya know? The good ones from the assholes."

I nodded, wishing I hadn't agreed to have a drink. Whoever these guys were, they knew my name, and that made me feel sick to my stomach. For the second time, I thought about calling Edge, but when I saw them get up and leave, I decided I'd just tell him about them later.

By the time I finished the one drink I'd been nursing, half of the people who had been at the bar when I got there had already left. The rest waved me off when I thanked them and said good night.

It was a foreign feeling for me to be part of a group. I'd never been before. In high school, I was a loner, and at the ranch kitchen, Tee-Tee spent so much time with just me, I felt like an outsider with the rest of the staff. It was probably my imagination that they resented me.

On the other hand, they never invited me to go to the Long Branch with them either.

When I got to the front door, Steel walked me out. "Edge will be here in a minute," he said as we waited a few feet away.

"I can walk home on my own," I told him when ten minutes went by without Edge showing up.

"You know I can't let you do that, Rebel."

"No one will know. You can tell Edge you walked me home."

"I value my life too much for that."

A few minutes later, Edge still hadn't shown up, but Christy walked outside. "You're still here?"

"Just waiting for my ride."

She looked between Steel and me. "Okay, well, good night." I watched her cross the street and go into one of the building's doors.

"She lives on the second floor," Steel explained, pointing when a light went on in one of the windows.

"Do you usually walk her over?"

He looked away, but I could see his cheeks flush. "Sometimes."

"You like her, don't you?"

The smile on his face shone through his eyes. "I do, but don't you go tellin' her that."

I crossed my heart. "Your secret is safe with me."

Edge's car pulled up a minute later, and he jumped out. "Sorry it took me so long to get here."

I didn't ask why, and he didn't offer.

Back at the house, we took a shower together and I crawled into bed. I knew I needed to tell him about the guys who came into the bar, but I was too exhausted to get into it. I would the next morning.

It wasn't until I stepped inside the kitchen the next morning and the sous-chef, Ben, handed me a cup of coffee that I realized I'd forgotten again to tell Edge about the men.

"Gonna be a long one today, Miss Lucy," he said, wiping his brow as I took the first sip of the best coffee I'd ever had. "You keep yourself hydrated now, ya hear?"

"I will, Ben. You know I always listen to you."

He stepped closer. "I heard there were some unsavories at the bar last night, wantin' to buy you a drink."

I didn't know what to say. That he knew, caught me off guard. "They thought I was someone else. It didn't turn into anything."

"That's not what Barney said. He told me that after you left, they came back, askin' all kinds of questions 'bout how long you've worked here, stuff like that."

Great. And I hadn't mentioned it to Edge. I thought about calling or sending him a text, but Susan walked in and I didn't have time. In the back of my mind, I prayed that whoever they were, they didn't show up again.

41

Edge

Last night, as I sat in my car waiting for Rebel, I watched two men who raised my hackles walk into her restaurant.

I thought about trying to get a photo for Decker to run, but I didn't want to ruin her time with her new friends. Instead, I decided to ask Steel to see if he could get me the restaurant's footage. If not, I'd have Decker hack in and get it anyway. There were times it was good to be a spy.

Just when I'd decided to get out of the car and make my way closer, the two men I'd seen earlier came back out and walked in my direction. I pulled my hat down farther on my forehead, zipped up my jacket, and then made my way off to the side and waited.

As they walked past, I heard one of the men say, "Fuckin' Rebel." His voice sounded so much like Possum's, I went on high alert. "If it weren't for her, Possum would still be alive."

I walked in the opposite direction and then circled back when they went into another bar. I waited just outside the entrance, a vantage point that allowed me to see where they were seated.

After they'd finished their beers, they paid their tab in cash, came outside, and walked south on Congress, farther away from me and, more importantly, from Rebel. I sneaked into the bar, hurried over, snatched one of the beer bottles, and took it into the men's room. Once there, I put it in a plastic bag. If facial recognition didn't turn up a hit on these guys, at least I'd have DNA from one of them.

I walked out of the men's room and then out of the bar without anyone appearing to have noticed me.

Since I knew Rebel would be waiting outside with Steel, I went around the block back to my car. On the way, I rang Deck, who said he'd come into Austin tomorrow morning to pick up the bottle after Rebel left for work.

"You want me to hang around for backup?" he asked after I explained what I'd seen and heard.

"Appreciate it, mate." Something in my gut told me I was going to need it.

When Rebel didn't mention the men either in the car or after we got back to the rental, I assumed she hadn't noticed them.

I found out differently this morning when Decker joined me to meet Steel for coffee. It was something I'd been doing every day after Rebel left for work.

"Tell us your side of what went down last night," I said to Steel once the three of us had our coffee.

He told us the bartender said the two men had first offered to buy Rebel a drink. "She goes by Lucy at the restaurant, so Barney—that's the bartender that was on last night—had no idea who they were talking about. When he quietly asked her if she knew who they were, she told him she didn't recognize either of them."

"She knew, then?"

When Steel confirmed she did, my ire rose. Why in the bloody hell hadn't she mentioned it?

"They came back in later. Pretty near closing time. Asked Barney a lot of questions about her."

"What did he tell them?" Decker asked.

Steel glared at him. "Jack shit."

"Good," muttered Deck.

"This morning, Ben, one of the sous-chefs, told Lucy that they'd come back. He said she was 'nervous as a chicken who saw a fox in the henhouse.' His words, not mine. He also said she tried hard to hide it."

"Anything else?"

"Yep. A little later, Ben said he saw her looking something up on her phone. He sneaked a peek and said she was looking at the public defender profiles."

My eyes met Deck's. Since it was Saturday night, Rebel would be working through the dinner hour. If these arseholes came back, I wanted to be ready.

"We're gonna need more backup," he said as though he'd read my mind.

I agreed.

"I'll see who's close."

"Hey, Deck—preferably Jagger and Rage."

"Right. Rebel doesn't know either of them."

By sundown, Decker and I were both in position, surveilling the perimeter outside the restaurant; Jagger and Rage were on their way inside.

"Something's about to go down," I said through the mouthpiece on my headset. "I can feel it."

"I can feel it too," Decker answered.

Two hours later, it did.

42

Rebel

"You okay?" asked Christy when she came to pick up the desserts I'd just plated for her table.

"Yeah, just busy."

She raised a brow.

We were busy. It was a Saturday night, and every seat had been full all night long. I'd lost track, but I heard someone say the tables had already turned three times and there was still a crowd waiting to be seated.

I'd been jumpy all day, and as hard as I tried to hide it, it was obvious my coworkers noticed. At least some of them.

"Are the two guys from last night what's worrying you?" she asked. Neither of us had time for this conversation, but if I didn't admit my fear to someone, I was going to break down.

"I think I might've recognized one of them," I said, making sure no one could hear us. Both men wore hats pulled down far enough that it had been hard to see their faces, but there was something familiar about the way one of them carried himself. I'd gone online earlier when Susan was on the phone, and pulled up the Hays County public defender page. One of the men who had been here the night before could very well have been John Lynch.

That alone was enough to make me lose my shit, but the fact that I hadn't told Edge about it, worried me even more.

"Lucy, a little help," one of the chefs hollered over to me and pointed to two bags of trash. The busboys and dishwashers were all busy, frantically trying to keep up. I was the next lowest on the "totem pole."

Christy squeezed my hand. "We'll talk later, but everyone out front is on the lookout for them."

I grabbed the bags and walked out the back door. The minute I did, every nerve ending on my body fired up. "You're getting yourself worked up about nothing," I muttered as I ran over to the dumpster and threw the trash bags in. My eyes surveyed the parking lot as I raced back to the door.

Just as I grabbed the handle to open it, I felt a hand go over my mouth.

"Make a sound, and I'll kill you right here and throw you in with the rest of the garbage." Something was poking me in the side, but it didn't feel like a gun. Maybe it was a knife, although it didn't feel like that either. Whatever it was, I wasn't going to risk trying to get away.

A split second later, I heard the distinct sound of a gun being cocked. When I squeezed my eyes closed, my first thought was of Edge and how I was about to die and I hadn't gotten the nerve to tell him I loved him.

"Let her go, asshole, or I'll blow your brains out!" I heard someone shout.

I stumbled to the ground when the man who'd had a hold of me let me go and took off running.

"Go, go, go!" I heard more voices shouting as another arm went around my waist and pulled me to my feet.

"I've got you, sweetness." *Edge. He was here.* I spun around and wrapped my arms around his neck as words began spilling out of me.

"Oh my God, I was so scared. I meant to tell you, and I forgot, and then we got so busy, and then…how did you know?"

"Come on, let's get you inside and out of the cold."

I looked behind us. "What's happening?"

Edge put a finger near his ear and opened the door with his other hand, escorting me back into the kitchen. "They've got 'em."

I took a deep breath, looked up, and saw the entire kitchen staff, and most of the waitstaff too, staring at me with their mouths hanging open. When I left to take the trash out, it had been chaos. Now it was dead silent.

Christy was the first to come out of shock and raced over to me. "Oh my God, what happened?"

Before I could answer, the back door opened and a uniformed policeman came inside. "We took two into custody, and I've got transport waiting for you out back."

"We don't have much time before the team and the other police officers arrive and all hell breaks loose," Edge said as he rushed me into the house after our ride over in the squad car.

Once we were past the doorway, he grabbed me by the back of the neck, pushed me up against the wall, and kissed me—long and deep and hard.

"I was so fucking worried about you." He looked into my eyes. "And you are in so much fucking trouble."

"Wait." I gripped his chin and looked into his eyes. "There's something else I have to tell you."

"Out with it."

"I love you, Edge."

He rested his forehead against mine. "How can I stay mad at you when you say that?" He winked and then brought his lips to mine, stopping right before they touched. "I love you too, my little Rebel."

Epilogue

Edge

I rolled over on the cabana bed and kissed Rebel's shoulder. "Getting hungry?"

"A little. I don't feel like moving, though."

"I'll go. Fancy Mexican?"

My beautiful little Rebel shook her head and answered the same way she always did. "I fancy English."

I kissed my way down her bare back, stopping at the edge of her bikini bottoms, and noticed her empty glass.

"Ready for another cocktail too?"

"I thought you'd never ask."

I walked over to the bar on the other side of the pool and looked out at the blue water of the Pacific Ocean. It wasn't easy to convince Rebel to take some time off, but after three long months, she'd finally agreed. But only after Susan threatened to fire her if she didn't. "Your apprenticeship is over, and your job will be waiting whenever you get back," she'd promised.

The man who had originally been assigned as Rebel's public defender, John Lynch, and his brother were in Hays County Jail, awaiting trial on a myriad of charges, including attempted kidnapping and attempted murder.

Evidently, they'd grown up with Possum and placed the blame for his death entirely on Rebel's shoulders, which couldn't be further from the truth.

I knew if Mac had anything to say about it, and he did, those wouldn't be the only charges the two men faced.

Two days after we arrived, we stood on the beach at sunrise, held hands, and Lucy "Rebel" Marks became my wife.

We'd been at our beachside bungalow for three weeks so far, and if we could stay another three, or longer, I'd be in heaven.

As I waited for the bartender to make us two more margaritas, I watched Rebel turn onto her back. I pulled out my mobile and rang hers. From where I stood, I could hear the ringtone I'd programmed in the day I gave it to her—Avici's "Addicted to You." She smiled and brought the mobile to her ear.

"Have I told you I love your tits, Mrs. Edgemon?"

"I think it's been at least an hour since you have."

"I do. I love the rest of you too."

As I watched, she raised her arms over her head.

"You're giving me naughty ideas."

"That was my intention."

"You know what to do, sweetness."

I signed for the drinks, placed an order for food to be delivered in an hour, and walked to the entrance of our bungalow where I knew my wife would be waiting on the bed, arms over her head, and legs spread.

Keep reading for a sneak peek
at the next book
in The Invincibles Series—
GRINDED!

1

Grinder

It was cold as hell tonight, which only exacerbated my pain and discomfort. Whoever said that what I experienced was psychosomatic, as some doctors did, should keep their opinions to themselves unless they'd suffered through the same trauma as people like me had.

It had been ten years since it last snowed in the hills outside of Austin, Texas. Ten years. The number was significant to me. It had also been ten years since I first met Pia Deltetto—the woman I believed might one day be my wife, the mother of my children.

I lived a lot of life in the years between then and now. Most of which I'd prefer to forget. There were days, weeks, and months when I wished I could forget Pia too, but she was too stubborn to let me. Her fiery spirit would force itself out of my subconscious until she was once again the star of my dreams—both awake and asleep.

Invariably, that meant I'd soon hear from her, as though my own spirit was connected to hers no matter where we were in the world.

Travel time to Florence was over fifteen hours, including a layover in Frankfurt. By the time I reached Tuscany, it would be Christmas.

Perhaps her gift to me would be one of forgiveness, although that was too much to expect or ask for.

Not long after I finally arrived at the farmhouse on the Deltetto's estate, I heard a knock at the door. I knew before I opened it that it was Pia. She could've walked right in—like she used to.

There was so much pain etched on her beautiful face, it broke my heart. I longed to see her smile, the one that drew me to her all those years ago.

She'd been crying, which didn't surprise me. Whatever she'd gotten herself involved in could ruin her. It could ruin her family too.

She looked into my eyes. *"Mylos."* The Italian pronunciation of my name on her tongue sounded like a song, one she'd sang from the day we met. "Why are you here?"

"I think you know."

About the Author

USA Today and Amazon Top 15 Bestselling Author Heather Slade writes shamelessly sexy, edge-of-your seat romantic suspense.

She gave herself the gift of writing a book for her own birthday one year. Forty-plus books later (and counting), she's having the time of her life.

The women Slade writes are self-confident, strong, with wills of their own, and hearts as big as the Colorado sky. The men are sublimely sexy, seductive alphas who rise to the challenge of capturing the sweet soul of a woman whose heart they'll hold in the palm of their hand forever. Add in a couple of neck-snapping twists and turns, a page-turning mystery, and a swoon-worthy HEA, and you'll be holding one of her books in your hands.

She loves to hear from my readers. You can contact her at heather@heatherslade.com

To keep up with her latest news and releases, please visit her website at www.heatherslade.com to sign up for her newsletter.

MORE FROM AUTHOR HEATHER SLADE

BUTLER RANCH

Kade's Worth
Brodie's Promise
Maddox's Truce
Naughton's Secret
Mercer's Vow
Kade's Return
Butler Ranch Christmas

WICKED WINEMAKERS
FIRST LABEL

Brix's Bid
Ridge's Release
Press' Passion
Zin's Sins
Tryst's Temptation

WICKED WINEMAKERS
SECOND LABEL

Beau's Beloved
Coming Soon:
Cru's Crush
Bones' Bliss
Snapper's Seduction
Kick's Kiss

ROARING FORK RANCH
Coming Soon:
Roaring Fork Wrangler
Roaring Fork Roughstock
Roaring Fork Rockstar
Roaring Fork Rooker
Roaring Fork Bridger

THE ROYAL AGENTS
OF MI6

Make Me Shiver
Drive Me Wilder
Feel My Pinch
Chase My Shadow
Find My Angel

K19 SECURITY
SOLUTIONS TEAM ONE

Razor's Edge
Gunner's Redemption
Mistletoe's Magic
Mantis' Desire
Dutch's Salvation

K19 SECURITY
SOLUTIONS TEAM TWO

Striker's Choice
Monk's Fire
Halo's Oath
Tackle's Honor
Onyx's Awakening

K19 SHADOW OPERATIONS
TEAM ONE

Code Name: Ranger
Code Name: Diesel
Code Name: Wasp
Code Name: Cowboy
Code Name: Mayhem

K19 ALLIED INTELLIGENCE
TEAM ONE

Code Name: Ares
Code Name: Cayman
Code Name: Poseidon
Code Name: Zeppelin
Code Name: Magnet

K19 ALLIED INTELLIGENCE
TEAM TWO
Coming Soon:
Code Name: Puck
Code Name: Michelangelo
Code Name: Typhon
Code Name: Hornet
Code Name: Reaper

PROTECTORS
UNDERCOVER

Undercover Agent
Undercover Emissary
Coming Soon:
Undercover Savior
Undercover Infidel
Undercover Assassin

THE INVINCIBLES
TEAM ONE

Decked
Edged
Grinded
Riled
Smoked

THE INVINCIBLES
TEAM TWO

Bucked
Irished
Sainted
Hammered
Ripped

THE UNSTOPPABLES
TEAM ONE

Furied
Married

COWBOYS OF
CRESTED BUTTE

A Cowboy Falls
A Cowboy's Dance
A Cowboy's Kiss
A Cowboy Stays
A Cowboy Wins